DOOM
655

Q SOLOMON

Privately Published Edition
Copyright © 2009
By Queshan Hayes

Please submit all inquiries to:

Queboy24@yahoo.com

I dedicate this book to all of those people in my life who believed in me, forgave me, trusted me and loved me...

-Q Solomon

A special thanks to Harlan, Nick, and T.J. for being the first people to read the book and offer suggestions, critiques, and praise.

Door 655

…..the saga begins.

1

I walked downstairs. I was both nervous and excited. I approached the blue door and just stood there. I had taken a long hot bath and felt refreshed and ready for the night. My skin was soft and smelled of vanilla and baby oil. I don't believe in cologne. My freshly trimmed facial hair was perfectly edged as if it was drawn on my face. I took a deep breath and I knocked.

My heart was beating uncontrollably as I heard the music coming from behind the door with the brass numbers "655" nailed above the peep hole. I waited. With my heart still racing, I knocked again. "I knew it, I knew it," I thought to myself as I turned to walk away. Before I reached the stairwell leading up to my apartment, door 655 creaked as it finally swung open and I could hear the music playing loudly. There in the doorway stood William, donned only in a towel and some bath sandals, with his cell phone propped to his ear with his shoulder.

"Craig? Where ya goin' man?" he asked with sincere concern. "I thought I heard you knockin'." Stopped in my tracks, my heart too almost stopped.

"Oh, I...I...I thought you had stepped out or something."

"Whatevah, man. I told you to come over and chill tonight, didn't I? I'm a man of my word."

A man he surely was. William was about 6'2". He stood on the thresh hold between the outside world and my fantasies. From head to toe, this man was beautiful. Not the practical beauty, but sheer sexual beauty. His muscular calves flexed as he stood there. His muscular thighs could not be hidden under the skimpy towel that he wore. His pubes, still wet and speckled with suds, made me bite my lower lip as I watched him finish up his conversation. His rippled upper body made me jealous with sensual desire. Then, there was that smile. His lips. Those lips. They weren't huge, yet they weren't thin. They were simply sexy. Simply....sexy.

"Hey, let me call you back," William barked into his cell phone, while holding one finger up as to say 'give me a minute.'

"Cuz I said so.....Yeah, I will.....Didn't I say I was? Aite, bye." He disconnected the call and smiled. "So, ya comin' in?" he asked, breaking my chain of inner thoughts. "Hell! Come on in," he said without waiting for my answer. He grabbed me and gave me a big bear hug, forgetting or not really caring that he was still wet. I had to control myself from getting an erection, despite feeling William's body pressed against mine.

"Its only water," he said with a grin. "Make yourself at home. I'll be out in a minute," he said as he disappeared deeper into the apartment, putting his cell phone down on the nearby end table. I sat on the couch taking in this new environment. I had never been in his apartment. Then my mind began to drift. I thought of all of the lonely nights when I listened. I was ashamed, but I had listened many times......

Coming home from work, I always passed William's door, door 655. This particular day as I passed the door I glanced at the numbers and wondered what went on behind that door. I knew that my young, dark, sexy neighbor entertained a lot of females as I had seen leave his apartment on several occasions. This day, my curiosity would be sufficed. I made my way to my apartment and routinely unlocked the top lock first and then the bottom. As I approached my desk, I noticed the flashing red light on my telephone, indicating that I had messages. Dropping my gym bag and briefcase, I pressed the button to dial my voicemail. I halfway listened as I sifted through my mail. It was a few calls from my mother sending her love and telling me how much she missed me. There was a call from an old college buddy and a couple of appointment reminders. As I came to the end of my messages, I heard what I first thought was knocking on my door. I stopped the messages and turned to go towards the front door. However, I soon realized that the source of the sound was not from my door, but it was coming from my bedroom.

A little puzzled, I went down the hall towards my room. I looked around, still puzzled. Then, I turned my head towards the far wall, just a few feet away from my bed. This was the source of the knocking. "What in the hell?" I whispered to myself. It wasn't knocking. The rhythm was too steady. Getting closer to the wall, I leaned my head against it and just listened. I soon heard voices and heavy breathing. The rhythm changed. The steady beat was now random with pauses and began to get louder and more forceful. The voices also increased in volume. It was now clear to me that it was two people involved in wild, passionate sex! It took only seconds for me to realize that it was not just anybody, but my most desirable neighbor below, William. He was fucking the hell out of whoever was moaning. Then, it happened. I slowly squatted down and pressed my ear even harder into the wall. It was difficult to hear because my racing heart was beating too loudly. But when the sex got very passionate, I could actually feel the vibrations of William's headboard banging against the wall. Then I heard it. I distinctly heard William's voice, moaning with desire.

"Yeah, Ohhh yeah. Baby yeah. Shit!" William huffed, full of breath. My imagination began to take over. I knew what William looked like with clothes on, but I quickly created my own image of what was under those clothes. And as I did this, my right hand slowly made its way into my loose fitting sweat pants. I closed my eyes tightly as I strained to listen. Once again, the banging got louder. The moans escalated. My hand became more intense. I could see it. I could see William's muscular ass jerking back and forth as he fucked whoever "she" was. I could see their fingers interlocked as the intensity of their lovemaking grew and grew. I saw the sweat on William's chocolate face. I saw William's manly feet digging into the sheets as he tried to go harder and deeper. My dick grew thicker and harder as this flick played in my head. William's cries and moans got louder. My hand got faster. William was about to orgasm. Shit, so was I. I sat there smiling, remembering like it was yesterday.

"So, what's up?" asked William as he interrupted my secret moment. Hiding my semi-erection, I placed my hands in my lap. I noticed William was now dressed. He wore some nylon basketball shorts and a basketball jersey. His skin was vibrant and glistening. He came over and just fell into the couch, inches from me. He switched the radio off and the television on. Absorbing all of this, I finally answered him. "Oh...nothing. Just working and trying to get the bills paid."

"I know that's right. I don't see you that much anymore. I know I've been busy with work, working out and city league basketball, but your ass been hiding!" he said as he flipped through the channels. He finally stopped on some violent movie that he recognized and got really excited. "Oh shit! I love this movie!" he said as he reached out and grabbed my leg catching me off guard. His touch sent a shock through my body.

"This movie is crazy as hell! There is this faggot, yo, that goes around killing all these people that used to dog him out in high school. I mean this bitch ass nigga is really crazy." My semi-erection immediately began to die down. My face began to heat up with disbelief, embarrassment, and fear.

How could William use that word? "What am I doing here?" I thought to myself. My mind began to race. William was really getting into the movie. He turned to see if I was enjoying it as much as he was. I wasn't and I was never good at hiding my feelings on my face.

"Hey man. Are you alright?" asked William.

"Oh...um..Yeah...yeah...I'm fine, just a little tired, I guess."

"Hey, we can chill another time if...."

"Oh no! I just need a little something to drink and I'll be fine. Can I have some water or something?"

"Oh, shit. I'm sorry, man. My mama raised me better than that. Let me get you something," he said as he got up and went to the kitchen. I watched him as he got up. It was obvious that he wasn't wearing any underwear. But how could I be thinking about dick at a time like this? Hell, I'm a man, that's how. William returned with a glass of orange juice.

"Here, man, I hope this is alright." As I began to sip, I realized that this juice was more than just juice. The harsh flavor of vodka hit me as the glass touched my lips.

"Um...thanks man. This is just what I needed," I said with a forced grin.

"I thought you would like it. I had a glass or two before my shower, so I'm in the zone, man." I nodded in agreement and sipped my drink wondering if this was going to be one of those crazy nights that I just sat and 'chilled' with one of my 'boys' all the while wanting him to grab me in his arms and tongue me down. Oh, the many nights in my hometown when my friends who were beautiful, athletic brothers had invited me over just to 'chill' and drink. The many fantasies that went through my head that I never had the nerve to pursue out of fear. Fuck it! I wasn't going to hold back tonight. I was going to make this fantasy with William a reality. I could feel it.

2

Why did he hug me so tightly wearing just a towel, making sure that I saw him half naked and making sure that I felt his half naked body? All I needed was a little more to drink and it would all fall into place. You see, like most people, when I drink, I become quite confident. But would it make me confident enough to make my move?

"Time for another drink, Craigy Craig! Shit, I just might have to get fucked up tonight. You gotta work tomorrow, Craig? Hell no! Tomorrow is Saturday and yo ass is off. I know yo schedule!" William said with a wink as he rose to fix another round of drinks.

"Um…Yeah. But I wanna hit the gym hard tomorrow. So, I can hang for a little while," I said as I gulped the remainder of my drink. "Hey, can I have another one, man?" I called out, remembering my plan.

"I was already on it, Craig. It might be a little strong though," William yelled back from the kitchen.

"That's cool, I need a strong one,"I responded without realizing I had said it out loud.

"What was that?" asked William.

"Oh, nothing, just talking to the T.V."

William returned with two tall glasses of vodka and maybe a splash of orange juice in each glass. He stumbled a bit as he flopped on the couch. The cups trembled in his hand as he tried not to spill any.

"Here, man, this one is yours," he said as he passed me a glass of cloudy orange-like liquid.

"You trying to kill me, William?"

"Just making you a man. Just making you a man," he said. He then took a sip. "Damn! This is some strong shit." And with that statement, he leaned further back into the couch as he began to really relax. He sat back and slowly, sensuously licked his lips. He stretched out his muscular legs. My eyes began to hurt because I tried to look at William while simultaneously pretending to watch television. It was straining my eyes. Then out of nowhere, William cocked his head back and let out a long, loud, manly growl of both comfort and intoxication. This gave me the opportunity to

9

scan his entire body without him noticing. And this is just what I did.

I started at his chin. I nervously stared at his perfectly square chin. His facial hair was black, course, and beautiful. It was bone straight. My eyes rolled across his Adam's apple that trembled as he swallowed every now and then. Then, to the chest hairs that were peeking out of the top of the basketball jersey that he wore. William had his right hand on his stomach with his shirt slightly lifted. My dick began to stiffen as I imagined my own hand in the place of his. Lower my eyes trailed and then they stopped. Halfway through their journey, they were thrown off course. I could not believe my eyes. There, between William's legs, was a raised area. Right there, against his left thigh was something that resembled a large cucumber, hidden behind those loose fitting shorts. I had not noticed this before. Of course I had seen it swinging when he walked, but it was not firm and as obvious as it was now. My mouth began to get dry as my own dick began to grow. I swallowed. I just wanted to reach out and just brush my fingers across it. But I wasn't trying to get killed anytime soon. So, my eyes stood there frozen on William's slightly aroused member. I didn't notice, but William had leaned his head back up. He locked eyes with me and looked down at his dick.

"Sorry about that man. I just get horny when I drink," he said as he reached down and grabbed his growing bulge in a way that almost made me explode. I could not believe that William had caught me. This awakened me from my daze. Now, I was both embarrassed and uncomfortable. Yet, my own erection lingered. William looked me in the eye. And then he looked down and saw that I was just as hard as he was.

3

What was there to say? We were two men sitting in a room with erections. Suddenly, William finally broke the silence. "I guess that shit makes you horny, too," he said as his eyes rolled back in his head and he chuckled.

"No, its you who makes me horny," I mumbled with a slurred laugh. Shit! Did I actually say that? Had those words truly escaped my deep down feelings and emerged from my slowly numbing lips? Apparently William hadn't heard me, or pretended not to hear me. He just sat back with his drink in his hand, head once again cocked back. Maybe two men with erections, 'chilling', was okay in the straight world. Then, there was that awkward silence when all time freezes and you sit there hoping that somebody, but not you, will make that first move. Your palms are sweating, your heart is racing and your mouth is dry. Then, it happened. I reached over with my trembling right hand and slowly laid it on William's left thigh. Lightly, but firm enough to be noticed. No movement from William. However, I could have sworn that William's, now fully erect penis jerked up with my touch. Yet, he sat there, still, with his head cocked back. Now with my heart still racing a mile a minute, I just let my hand linger there for what seemed like an eternity.   Should I move it up further, or just wait for William's reaction? All that I wanted to do was let just two fingers, just two, brush across that huge bulge in his shorts. I was only inches, just inches away. Encouraged by the alcohol, my now steady hand inched its way up William's thigh. If I had not been moving my hand myself, I wouldn't have known that it was moving. I was moving it just that slowly and cautiously. I would not spoil this moment. I was now closer. Then, even closer. I was so close that I could feel the heat that rose from William's crotch. One more inch. Just one more. Almost... Almost there! William's head slowly rolled up, he leaned forward, and was standing—all in one movement.

"I...I think its time to call it a night, man....I...I got a lot to do tomorrow," he said as he struggled to keep his balance and hide his now rock hard dick that formed a pyramid in his shorts. He couldn't look me in the eye, nor could I look him in his. My eyes were in another place. Then, I snapped back to realize what was happening.

"Uhhhh...um..Ok...I was just...I...I'm sorry William," I said as I struggled to stand up. "I didn't mean to...um.."

"Nah, man, its ahight."

"No, let me explain...I..." I said as I stumbled over my own feet. William reached out to catch me before I fell. I completely lost my balance and William caught me, only to press our bodies together. Chest to chest, I finally felt William's dick jab me in my thigh. It slid to the side and pressed closer up against me as William caught and held me there. My dick ached as it melted into William's tight muscular thigh. I let out a gasp of drunken ecstasy. I could have exploded at that single moment, but my mixed feelings would not allow me to reach climax. What felt like hours were merely seconds. William just stood there holding me pressed against him. His own dick twitched against my leg. Was this my opportunity? I slowly and sensuously slid up his body to stand straight up and firmly on my feet. Suddenly, William's pelvis began to grind itself into my thigh. First, in slow, gentle circles, then in hard circles, so much so that I could feel every inch of his dick. Yet, we never made eye contact. My face was barely over his shoulder, facing the door. William faced the TV screen and closed his eyes tightly as his own mind left the room and became overwhelmed with thoughts, fears, nightmares, and memories.....Yes, memories.....

*****

"Come on Uncle Wes, I'm gonna be late for practice," William, age 17 pleaded.

"I already told you boy that your Mama is coming home soon, so come on in here," his uncle pleaded as he sat across the guest bed in some loose fitting slacks, his erection slowly growing. William slowly put down his basketball and took off the long key chain he wore around his neck. He walked into the small guest room and instinctively closed the door behind him. He now stood in the room that his uncle stayed in each summer that he came to visit. William's heart raced, his palms sweated, and his knees shook. But what confused him was the fact that his own dick began to grow. He was a young man who had had sex with quite a few young females, but now, in this small room, smelling of Polo Sport

12

and Irish Spring soap, his dick began to rise for another man, his uncle.

"Come here boy," his Uncle said, full of breath as he reached down and lightly caressed his own growing dick. William could see it growing as it formed a small tent in his pants. He walked past the dresser and around to the other side of the bed. He made sure that his oversized shirt hid his own growing erection. His uncle slowly stood up, inches away from William.

"Come on and give your uncle a hug, boy. I haven't seen you in years," he said with a grin, when he had just seen him this morning. William hated it when his uncle joked around like this as if it made the situation any more comfortable. It was funny when he was younger, but now it was just dumb. Inches from William, he stretched out his muscular arms. William inched toward him until he could feel his uncle's dick on his upper right hip.

"Hug me, boy," he said a little forceful, yet sensuously. William slowly lifted his arms and lightly placed them on his uncle's back.

"Thatta boy," he said. He then squatted and grinded himself into William's body. He started slowly in circular motions, moaning and grunting.

"Yeah…boy..yeah..you feel that..? You feel that, boy?" his uncle quizzed. William looked past his uncle's shoulder and out the tiny window. He thought that if he closed his eyes and took himself to another place, his own erection would go down. But it didn't.

"Yeah boy…you like that, don't you? You like it…I feel it…You like that don't you boy?" William just closed his eyes and kept his arms loosely draped around his uncle's waist. But something was different. His own dick was now rock hard. It was at full throttle. The harder his uncle grinded, the closer William felt he was getting to climax. And before he knew it, he was on the edge…He was about to orgasm. Shit! This had never happened before. What was going on? William's once loose grip had subconsciously evolved into a tight embrace. He began to tightly grasp his uncle's muscular back, pulling him closer. His uncle, amazed, stopped his own movement and held William in awe. William began to grind harder and harder.

"Uncle Wes…Uncle Wes…Uncle…Oh, oh..ohhh!"
he grunted as his dick exploded and he trembled and jerked.
His stomach convulsed over and over until he felt the hot
liquid ooze in his boxer shorts. His uncle, now in complete
and utter amazement, held William back by his shoulders and
looked him in his eyes. William stood there, out of breath,
eyes clenched closed, chest heaving, stomach convulsing. His
breathing slowly became normal and he slowly lifted his eyes
to meet his uncles'. They stood there looking at each other in
silence.

"Go on boy. You gonna be late for practice," his
uncle said in a solemn, almost guilty voice. William lowered
his hands, took a few steps back and disappeared out of the
room. He had never run so fast before in his life. Down the
steps, up the street, and into the park. He stood with his back
against a tree. Tears streaming, he clenched his fists and all
that escaped his throat was a hoarse, shrill: "Nooooooo!"

"William!?? William! William!!!! What is it?" I
shouted as my heart raced from fear after William began to
yell and forcefully pushed me away. William stood, shaking,
and out of breath. His eyes were wild and racing. They
searched the entire room as if he didn't know where he was.
They finally landed back on me. He then looked down at his
own shorts and saw the wet circle that had mysteriously
appeared. He then looked me in my eyes, chest still heaving.

"I think I better leave. I'll talk to you later," I said as I
turned to the door and left William standing there like a
zombie. Soon, I was on the other side of door 655. I stood
there a minute. I was dazed, confused, still horny and a little
buzzed. Although I had just closed the door on a shattered
fantasy, I knew I had opened another door. As I started to
head upstairs to my apartment, I turned back to look at the
numbers on the door once more. There was something wrong,
but I wouldn't press the issue. Not yet anyway.
Because I knew William's type. You just wake up tomorrow
and act as if nothing happened. You make eye contact, but not
too much. You smile. You say, "What's up" You give the
'homeboy handshake' with a hug and you go about your
business. That's what I decided to do. But something stuck in
my mind. Something that I could not and would not let go.
Who was Uncle Wes? I had heard stories of cheating lovers

calling out another person's name during sex, but not calling out a family member's. I had distinctly heard William say 'UNCLE' Wes. Was this some sick fantasy that William had? I would soon find out.

4

I made my way up the flight of stairs and entered my apartment. I stumbled a bit, but was glad that I was finally in the comfort of my own environment. "Oh well," I thought to myself as I walked into my bedroom. Still slightly buzzed, I undressed and put my clothes away.

"What in the hell am I doing? This guy invites me over, then kicks me out when I try to get me some," I laughed as I turned on the water for a quick shower. I stepped in and let the warm water flow over my body. I had not reached climax with William. But now, now I had a hot image. I had felt it all. Although I hadn't had enough time to get my hands on that muscular ass, I did feel enough to create the perfect image. I lathered my entire body with soap. I tilted my head back and lightly caressed my nipples. My body was sculpted. I was no body builder, but I had run track in high school. My toned body glistened as the steamy water caressed every cut and crevice. I rubbed my hands through my pubic hair and played with my dick until it was once again rock hard. I juggled my balls lightly, just to arouse me even more. I slowly, loosely wrapped my fingers around my entire shaft. I began stroking it gently as visions of William danced through my head. At first, I barely touched it, so that every light, random touch sent a sexual jolt through my entire body. Soon, not able to take it anymore, I grabbed my dick and began stroking with such a force that water and suds flew against the tiles and shower curtain. I could feel every vein. The sound of water and skin, sliding back and forth echoed in the shower. My knees began to bend. I couldn't take it anymore. The hot water, soap, and warm hand created the perfect friction. Finally.....

"Shit!..Yeahhhh....Shit!, William, Oh William!!!" I moaned as I shot a stream of thick cream all the way to the other end of the shower. I cleaned myself up, rinsed, and turned off the water. I dried, being careful with my now sensitive, yet satisfied, member. I slid into my favorite black boxer briefs. But before climbing in bed, I went over to my wall and pressed my head against it. I listened. Nothing. Just silence. I smiled to myself and climbed into bed. My shower session was the perfect cure for my insomnia. On the edge of sleep and consciousness, my eyes rolled back. In the blackness of night, sleep took over. Then out of nowhere, my phone rang.

"What the fuck?!," I grumbled as I snatched up the receiver. I rolled over just to see that it was 1 AM.

"Hello!??!" I barked into the phone.

"Hey man, whassup. It's me, William."

I froze as I sat up in bed. I was completely speechless. The words just would not come. The silence was so thick that the operator wanted to jump in.

"Hey, you there, man?"

"Um...uh...yeah, I'm here," I said, finally able to speak. I couldn't believe William had actually picked up the phone and dialed my number. The alcohol slowly lost its affect on both of us and we were both thinking a little clearer now. Me in my bed wearing only boxer briefs. William was standing in his kitchen with a new pair of loose fitting basketball shorts, pacing back and forth. His heartbeat shook his whole body and he just knew that I could hear it over the phone. It took all of his inner strength to sound calm and cool as if nothing was wrong.

"I....I was just calling to make sure you got in okay, man," he stammered.

Hell, it was only a few feet away. What?! Was a meteor going to come flying down and strike me unconscious? 'Did I get in okay?' What in the hell?! Yet, I decided to play along.

"Oh...yeah, I made it just fine. No deadly meteorites or drive-by thugs out to kill me tonight," I said as I rolled my eyes.

"Oh, you're the comedian tonight, huh?" William blurted out with a forced, nervous laugh. "Anyway, man, that was some strong shit, huh? I'm finally chilled out, now. I don't even remember you leaving. When did you dip out, man?"

And with those words, I knew. My heart almost stopped. My eyes closed tightly. I almost gasped. It took everything in my soul not to lose it. So, that was the plan: We were drunk and we don't remember shit! I could not believe my ears.

"Hey, William, it's really late, and I've got to get some sleep. Talk to you tomorrow?" I said as I rubbed my temples.

"Sure, man. Later." And the conversation was over. Dial tone.....

Although I had seen the whole scene before, it was much harder to swallow when you became an actual actor in it. Alright, you get drunk, but who would forget what just happened hours ago? I knew the answer immediately after I thought it.

"A confused closet case," I thought. "Shit, it's almost 2 A.M. Fuck this shit! Fuck it!" I grumbled as I rolled over and pulled up my covers. I was exhausted, but couldn't sleep. My mind was full of questions.

5

William hung up the phone and paced back and forth in his kitchen. He stopped to look into his refrigerator. Nothing was there.

"Why in the fuck you always gettin me in trouble," he said as he looked down and grabbed his crotch. "Shit!" he said as he slammed his fist on the kitchen counter. What had he done? It was like he was in a dream, a bad dream. He had invited a neighbor to his apartment. They chilled, drank some alcohol, watched some T.V. and ended up rubbing dicks. He stopped pacing and decided that it was time for bed, but he could not get Craig out of his head. He walked towards his bedroom.

"What in the fuck am I supposed to do now? How am I supposed to sleep on some shit like this? Fuck you Uncle Wes! Fuck you!" he said as he slammed the door of his bedroom. He sat across his bed with his head cupped in the palms of his hands. Just then, he had a thought. He stood up and walked over to his nightstand. He scanned through his programmed phone list. After a few seconds of scanning, he finally pressed the DIAL button.

"Hello?" a familiar voice answered after only the second ring.

"Yeah, whassup with you? What you doin' up so late? I thought I was going to have to leave you a message," William said in a sexy voice with a touch of thug flavor. After a second or two of silence, the voice responded.

"Because. I...I knew you were going to call me tonight. I felt it....I felt it deep between my legs," the voice said with a laugh so sexy that Janet Jackson would have paid to include it in one of her sexy interludes. After tonight's events, William was confused, angry, mad, but still horny—all of the ingredients for wild, passionate sex.

"So when you comin' over?" he asked.
--Dial tone.
William held the receiver to his ear and smiled for a second. He knew what this meant. It meant he was getting some tonight. If there was any added conversation after that single, most important question, he knew it meant that she was either occupied or had an early day the following morning and he

would have to service himself. But neither of these were the case tonight. She had hung up. She was on her way.

6

Cicely was her name and doing the nasty was her game. She was a caramel colored sister with shoulder length, permed hair. She was indeed beautiful. Her make-up was always flawless and her wardrobe fierce. William had met her out at a local club one night and boned her the same night and the following afternoon and many times after that. Craig had heard them. She was on her way to get the ride of her life.

William looked at the clock.

"Damn! She'll be here any minute," he mumbled as he threw a towel into his closet where his dirty clothes had piled up. He jumped into the shower and turned on the water. Soon, he was foamy with soap and rinsed clean in less than ten minutes. He reached for a towel and wrapped it around his waist. Just as he was reaching for a Q-tip, he heard a knock at his door. Although he had just had an unanticipated orgasm with Craig, he was ready again. The thought of Cicely standing at his door in only a trench coat and black pumps, her usual freak wardrobe, made his still sensitive dick swell again. He smiled as he caught a glimpse of himself in the mirror.

"Fuck that nigga upstairs. I'm gonna get me some pussy tonight," he said as he turned off all of his lights in his bedroom. He reached over and lit two vanilla candles. He checked his drawer in the nightstand. Yep, his condoms were there. Then, he suddenly got an idea. Instead of drying himself off, he wanted to add the perfect effect and decided to be wet when he answered the door. The water made his muscular chest appear even more massive and cut. He turned to go to the door when another little dirty thought entered his mind. He dropped the towel. He again heard knocking. This time it was a quicker, impatient knock.

"I'm coming, I'm coming, damn," he mumbled. "You're gonna love this'" he said to himself. He was so excited that he didn't even check the peep hole. He leaned against the wall in a 'boy-next-door-Boris Kodjoe' pose, hard dick and all. He turned the knob and dramatically opened the door as if to say 'TA-DAH!'.

There in the door way I stood; breathless. The vision before my eyes was breath taking.

"Hey William…..um…wassup." William could not believe it! It was me!

7

Two men standing, one naked and one wishing that he was naked too. William in all of his glory; cut, muscular, leaning to one side with an erection that pointed straight at me. I stood on the other side of the threshold with a nervous grin, some shorts, and some sports sandals--- eyes locked on William's engorged, beautiful, chocolate stick. I could have sworn that I had subconsciously licked my lips.

"Oh shit!" William said as he quickly closed the door. He didn't mean to slam it in my face. It was a reflex. He then cracked it open just enough to stick his head through.

"Hey, man. Give me a minute, ahite?"

"Sure," I said, trying to hold back a smile that began to take over my face. William again closed the door and ran back into his bedroom to put on some shorts, all the while, I stood outside holding on to that once in a lifetime centerfold image of him standing there naked. All that I could do was whisper to myself, "Sweet Jesus!" as I shook my head. I stood there for a moment with my arms crossed, knowing that I now had an image to use for later solitary activities. In a matter of seconds, William was back at the door.

"Umm, come in man," he said as he opened the door wider to let me pass through. I walked in and stood by the couch where all of this had started. William slowly closed the door as he thought to himself, "Ohhh shit…"

"Look William…." I began. "I just couldn't sleep….I…I…don't know where to begin and I don't know what to say. I just wanted….I just needed…to…to…come and talk to you."

"Hey Craig…um…why don't you have a seat, man?"

"Oooooh No!….Ohhhh No….That's how this shit got started. I'm just gonna stand right here. Yeah, just stand right here until we get this handled," I said pointing down at the spot where I was standing.

"Ahite man, suit yourself," William said as he leaned against the door. He stood there looking at me, his head barely raised, his eyes like an innocent lamb. Then, there was that silence again.

"William, I know that a lot has happened in the past couple of hours, but we can handle this, right?" William stood there and thought for a few seconds. Then, as calm as a breeze, he said, "What are you talking about, Craig?"

"What am I talking about?!! What am I talking about?!!! You know damn well what I'm talking about," I exploded.

"Calm down, Craig. I'm not yelling, so I would appreciate it if you didn't yell at me," William said as he switched positions to lean his back against the wall and fold his arms.

"I've got neighbors and I don't need you waking them up."

"Fuck you and fuck your fucking neighbors, William!"

"Come on Craig, you really need to calm down or leave, man," he said with a little force.

"...Or what? You gonna kick me out? Or...What?...Beat my ass. What?!!!"

"Craig?!! Come on, man! It's not that serious. I'm just saying maybe you need to go back upstairs, calm down, and come back and talk to me like an adult."

"An adult? An adult?!!" I shouted. "An adult would face the facts, William. An adult would realize that he can't use alcohol as a fucking scapegoat. An adult would realize that he's a fucking faggot!"

And with those words, the whole atmosphere changed. The temperature in the room rose, heartbeats pounded so loudly that the walls shook. Then, there was William's expression. No longer an innocent lamb. No, it was pure evil, now. His forehead revealed a vein that danced across his entire head. He squinted his eyes and inhaled deeply, nostrils flaring. His once loosely folded arms, turned into two bars of steel with two tensed fists at both ends.

"What the fuck did you say?" Silence..... "What...in the fuck...did you say, Craig?" William repeated, pausing after each word. I noticed the change in William. So, I felt that it was in my best interest to remain silent. So I stood there, breathing heavily, chest still heaving from my prior outburst. Then, William snapped. He completely snapped. No longer leaning against the wall. No longer the innocent eyes of a lamb. No longer William. Now, just inches away from my nose. Now, with eyes of the devil himself. Now, some creature from the gates of hell, his wrath unleashed.

"What in the fuck did you say? Who in the fuck do you think you are? Just who do you think you are coming down here telling me you know who the fuck I am? Huh? Huh? You don't know me, Craig! You come into my fucking house and tell me some lame ass shit like this. Yeah, I did it. I did it! I rubbed dicks with yo ass. Shit, I ain't denying that. But I ain't no fucking faggot! You hear me? Do you hear me?" he said while pointing his finger into my chest. I had indeed heard every word. William's rampage had put a fear in my heart that I had never experienced.

"Now, you can say what ever the fuck you wanna say, but you ain't gonna call me no faggot in my own house! Look at me!! Look at me!! I'm a fuckin' man, nigga!! I play sports, I watch sports. I play basketball every fucking day with other men! I like pussy nigga! Pussy!! I got a fucking dick!! And I'm a fucking man!!…..You know what…? Get the fuck out!" he said matter-of-factly as he pushed me a little too hard, causing me to lose my balance and fall onto the couch, catching him by surprise.

Now there were two things that I would not stand for. Liars make my blood boil and negative physical contact made my adrenaline bubble. And William had just crossed one of those lines. In one swift movement, I was back on my feet and all in his face.

"What!? Because you're a man, you think you can push me around?"

"Hey man, I'm sorry. I didn't mean to push you down," he said, genuinely apologetic. He reached out to grab my arms.

"Get your hands off me!!" I said as I pushed his hands away. "Just because I like men, you think that makes me less of a man than you THINK you are? Huh?"

"Come on Craig, let's just drop it!" he pleaded.

"No…No, William. We are both men! And that's something you will never accept! I'm a fucking man, too!"

"I never said that you weren't a man. I was just letting you know that I wasn't a faggot. I know you are a man, Craig. I know that. I'm sorry if I made you feel any less. I'm really sorry that I pushed you, man," William begged. I was still breathing like a racehorse, but I decided to accept his apology. My feelings began to calm down in the silence. William realized that I was indeed a man. And I realized that I had disrespected him with a word that I, myself hated and swore that I would never use.

"Come on, man. It's not all that serious. We just both pushed each other's buttons," William said as he stepped back to walk away.

"So what is it really, though?" I asked. William closed his eyes and shook his head.

"I don't know, man. I just don't know. I mean…I…I tried, I tried to…I wanted to…I…." And slowly tears began to stream down his beautiful face. My heart immediately became heavy and I wished that I could take back all the hurtful words I had just expressed. I wanted to reach out to him, but didn't know if I should. I decided to take the chance and slowly reached out and put my hand on his right shoulder.

"Come on, man. Talk to me," I pleaded.

"Man, it's just so…so fucked up. My mom…I mean she didn't know. She couldn't have known."

"Know what, William? Know what?"

"My uncle Wes..He..he…" And it immediately hit me like a load of bricks why William had called out his Uncle's name during our incident.

"Did he touch you William?" And with that question, William's manly tears increased and became a fountain. He was no longer a man, but a scared, confused child, crying out for help. I reached out and hugged him tightly. And there we stood in a tight embrace; William sobbing and my heart crying, too. We were both men, yet at this moment, I somehow was more of a man than William could ever imagine.

Meanwhile, outside, Cicely parked her car. She smelled of expensive perfume and apple body spray. She checked her lips and hair as she opened her car door. Dressed in only black pumps and a black trench coat, she stepped out of her car. She pressed her remote key and her headlights flashed to confirm that her car was secured. She licked her lips one last time as she dropped her keys in her coat pocket and chewed Spearmint gum. As she walked, her perfume left a trail of a sexy aroma. The sexy, erotic sound of her heels clicked and echoed as she entered William's breezeway.

William's door was slightly cracked. This would often happen when he didn't lock it after closing it. It would sometimes ever so slightly spring back open. As Cicely approached the door, she inhaled deeply and smiled as she envisioned riding William's beautiful, massive dick. She reached out to knock. As she did so, the door slowly opened to a scene that almost made her collapse. There was William in an embrace with another man. She recognized the man. It was William's neighbor from upstairs.

"What the fuck is this? William, is this that faggot you told me about from upstairs?! Oh hell no!" she said as she rolled her eyes and flipped her hair. "I can't believe this shit. I hope you don't think I'm gonna let some faggot fuck me!"

I looked at her and my heart immediately broke into pieces as anger began to replace the compassion that I was just feeling for William. William looked at her then back at me. I looked William in the eye and pushed him away. Almost in tears, I walked towards the door.

"Oh, the little gay boy jealous?" said Cicely in a mocking baby talk tone as I walked towards the door. I stopped at the door, just inches from her face. I looked her dead in the eye and said, "Look, bitch, I have never hit a female in my life, but I'm always taking applications for the first. So if you ever…..ever call me a faggot again, you've got the fucking job! I wouldn't fuck your nasty ass if it was the answer for eternal life" and I pushed her aside and vanished into the night. Cicely turned away from me and looked back at William.

"What the fuck was that about?" she asked. William just stood there shaking his head in disbelief. "What…Are you a fucking homo, now, too?" she smirked with one eye brow raised. Williams head stopped shaking and he slowly raised his eyes to her..

"Get the fuck out!"

8

Cicely looked at William and gasped. She couldn't believe that William was turning her down. She would not be rejected. Her expression immediately transformed into one of pity.

"I'm sorry baby. I...I didn't mean it," she whined as she moved closer to him. "I just saw you and....and him, and... I...I got jealous and...."

"Jealous?!!! Jealous!?? What the fuck you got to be jealous about?" William interjected. "That punk was upset about some shit goin' on in his life and I was being cool and shit."

"I know baby, I know."

"Shit, I ain't no heartless mothafucka,"

"I know baby, I know," pouted Cicely as she wrapped her arms around William and caressed his broad, manly chest. He was still in his own angry world. Cicely leaned closer to him and felt his heart racing against the side of her face. Just as she was getting comfortable, she was suddenly jerked up and away from him. He pushed her back and firmly held her by her shoulders. He looked her in her eyes.

"Don't you ever call me a fucking faggot again! Do you hear me?"

"Umm...yeah, I hear you William. I hear you! You're hurting me..." she mumbled as her eyes became wild with fear and shock.

"Oh....Im...Im sorry," he said as he loosened his grip, realizing how forceful his grip was on her. "I just wanted to make sure you understood me."

"I...I understand," she said, her heart now racing. She didn't understand why he was getting so upset. She said what she said because she was really jealous. Was there truly something behind the scene that she had just witnessed? She decided to put it out of her mind and go with her original agenda; to get William naked, taste every inch of him, and then ride him until he exploded. She looked up into his eyes, pressed herself closer to him once again and whispered in his ear.

"Hey, baby, Im sorry. So, so, so sorry. Can you forgive me?" she pouted. At first William still had a far off look in his eyes. But soon, he came back to reality and remembered his purpose. He slowly lifted his arms and loosely wrapped them around Cicely. He felt every curve. Her breasts pressed against his manly chest as she let out a sigh of pleasure. William leaned his head down, pressed his sexy lips against hers and immediately put his tongue deep into her mouth. Their tongues rolled around until William's dick began to rise and press against Cicely's upper thigh. She felt his manhood and her own nipples began to harden. William's hands moved down her back and teased her as they stopped at that crucial point where her ass meets her back. Lingering there for just a second, his hands then made their way to her ass. He first caressed each cheek with both hands softly, gently lifting her trench coat. Then, as his tongue went deeper, he grabbed her roughly and pulled her so close to him that she felt every inch of him. He slowly squatted and grinded his manhood into her body. Soon, his hands were everywhere. Up and down her back, running through her hair, back to her ass, where they stayed. She withdrew from his mouth and made her way to his neck. She licked and sucked his shoulders. Her hands also began to explore his body. Feeling each muscular, solid part of William, her arousal became even more intense. She was so anxious that she went straight for that muscular ass. She could have died at that moment. She loved to feel William's manly, muscular, chocolate ass. She felt that he wore no underwear. Her hands tensed as she tried to fill each palm with William's ass cheeks. It was solid. She went lower and cupped each cheek as William grinded himself deeper into her body. She was in ecstasy as she felt him tense up into a solid mass of sexual steel. In a matter of minutes, they were both naked. Their bodies pressed together, their heads locked by their tongue play. William lifted Cicely off her feet. She straddled his waist as he carried her to the bedroom. His two candles were projecting sexual shadows on his walls and ceiling.

"Damn, baby," William moaned. "It's been a long time...You taste so good. I'm sorry I grabbed you. Can you forgive me," he said in between kisses. He laid Cicely down lightly. He licked her from head to toe, stopping in all of the right places. He was ready. She was ready. He reached over and pulled out a condom as his free hand massaged her breasts. With one leg on the bed and one foot on the floor, he rolled the condom on. Just the touch of his own hand made him precum, just a little. He stroked his huge dick just three times before he went to action. First, in slow smooth thrusts he went in and out. Cicely moaned and groaned.

"Oh William…yeah baby…I like that…"she said. William interlocked his fingers with hers and flattened her outstretched arms against the bed. His slow, smooth strokes evolved into hard, animalistic thrusts.

"Yeah, baby….You like that…Yeah, you like that right there. Damn this shit is good," he moaned as he went in and out, in and out, in and out. Faster and harder…Harder and faster. "I'm a fuckin' man!"

"Yeah, yes you are, baby," she moaned.

"Shit! Shit!…Ohhh Shit," he yelled as he fucked the hell out of Cicely. She was moaning louder, on the edge of orgasm. Then all of a sudden, William reached his point.

"Damn baby, Dammmmmmmn!" he growled as his body shook and jerked.

Upstairs, I sat by the wall. I had heard the familiar headboard banging and wanted to confirm my hunch. Yes, William and that woman were fucking. As I heard what I figured was William's orgasm, I took my ear away from the wall. Staring into space, a single tear rolled down my cheek. My heart grew heavy as I pictured William with…with…her! I saw them. I saw her.

"Why are you doing this to me, God? Why?" Yet, I realized I was doing it all to myself. I cried a few more tears, then wiped them away. I picked myself up and climbed into bed. I looked up at my ceiling as I pulled my covers up over my chest.

"Forgive me, Lord." And I was off to sleep.

9

William laid there, out of breath. Cicely laid there beside him, numb and confused. The sex was good, but he had never sexed her like that before. He was an animal, she thought to herself. What was behind all of that anger and tension? William just stared up at the ceiling.

"William? William?" Cicely repeated. He still layed there looking into space. Cicely raised up and looked him directly in the eyes. "William!"

"Yeah...what?...What?" he said, finally snapping out of his trance.

"I've gotta go. I can't spend the night,"

"Yeah..ok...whatever."

"WHATEVER!?, whatever? What do you mean, 'whatever'?"

"You said you had to go, so go. I can't stop you."

"Nigga, you are really trippin," she said as she got up. She put on her shoes, went into the living room, wrapped herself in her coat and was gone. She slammed the door.

"Dumb bitch," William mumbled. He turned over and looked at his phone. No matter how much sex he had, he still felt Craig's pain. But he couldn't call him. He wouldn't.

Meanwhile, my apartment was silent. Suddenly, the silence was broken. My phone rang.

"Shit, who in the fuck," I grumbled as I reached for the phone. "Oh no, not again," I said as I rolled back over and decided not to answer it. It rang one last time and my answering machine picked up. On the machine was the sexiest voice I had ever heard. It made my heart skip a beat.

"Hey, Craig....It's me, Tony. Just callin' to say...um....Hi....and that I was...ummm, thinkin' about you and wanted to come over tonite and see you. So when you get this message, no matter what time it is, give me a buzz." And he was gone.

Did my ears deceive me? Was I dreaming? Was that really Tony? I knew that it was and so did my body. Right now, it ached for what Tony could give. I picked up the phone and Tony's number came to me as I dialed the first three digits. The receiver was picked up on the first ring.

"Hello?" My throat got dry. "Ummm….Tony?"

"Yeah, is this you, Sexy?"

"Yeah, its me…Got your message."

"No doubt. No doubt. So I'm on my way?"

"Are you?"

"Be there in about twenty minutes."

"Later," and I hung up the phone. I sat there frozen.

Tony. Tony Jackson was a man that had everything that one could ask for, sexually that is. His body was like a Roman God, dipped in chocolate. His legs were strong, firm, smooth and powerful. And when he wore his Calvin Klein baggy jeans, he let them sag just a little. His muscular ass held them in place. He was an older guy with a sexual appetite that was almost unhealthy. I liked older guys, especially beautiful ones, like Tony.

Tony made that familiar journey across town to my complex. He parked his car and stuffed his hands in his pockets as he walked under the parking lot lights. He walked up the stairs with a semi erect penis. Finally, approaching the familiar door, he knocked. In minutes, I opened the door and stood to the side to allow him to pass. He brushed by me. I inhaled deeply as the mixed scent of Irish Spring soap and Polo Sport filled my nostrils. I closed my eyes tightly and savored the moment. Tony went straight to the bedroom. I followed him. No words were spoken. We both stood on opposite sides of the bed. Tony lifted his shirt and revealed a chiseled chest. He then unbuttoned his pants and unlaced his boots. It was all like a silent ritual. He then broke the silence as each boot hit the floor with a manly thud. His jeans fell to the floor with a jingle as his belt buckle landed. His concealed weapon bulged out of his white boxer briefs. I, too, was aroused. Without any direction, Tony pulled the sheets back and slid beneath them. I turned off the lights and got in on the other side. I had set the CD player to come on in a matter of minutes and it did.

Through my surround sound speakers emerged Cassandra Wilson's sexy voice. It was the Love Jones soundtrack. "Sexing 101" is what I called it. Tony and I had our first encounter while this CD played at Tony's house. In the darkness, Tony smiled as he recognized the soundtrack. Soon, he reached out and caressed my shoulder. I had my back towards him. At first, his touch was soft and gentle. Then it

32

began to get a little rough and he began to grind and massage my shoulders with just enough force to send chills down my back. This caused me to instinctively move closer to him. Now, only inches from him, I felt his breath on the back of my neck. It sent a wave through my spine that made my toes curl. Then, I made that crucial move. I arched my back so that my ass melted into his now rigid dick. He moaned just a little as my firm, bubble ass pressed against his dick. He reflexively arched his back to press his dick harder into my round cheeks. Tony could not resist. He reached completely around me and held me tightly. He spooned my body as we both began to grind and gyrate. Suddenly, I felt his sexy, moist tongue lick my ear lobe. From my ear lobe, his tongue made its way to my neck. I reached down and grabbed my own dick. I began to stroke it slowly as I pushed my ass further back into Tony's body. In minutes, our legs were wrapped into each other. He grabbed my busy hand and pulled it away. He then took over. For a man, his hands were soft and gentle. He stroked me slowly and gently. I reached my now free hand behind my head and grabbed him behind his neck as he gently bit and sucked on my neck.

"Yeah, yeah ..." I moaned. Tony then pulled my hand away, reached over and forcefully flipped me around to face him, as if it was some type of wrestling move. He grabbed my head and pulled it close to his own. His full lips wrapped themselves around my lips as he forced that strong tongue deep into my mouth. He then reached over and grabbed my ass and pulled my body even closer to his. There we laid grinding dicks. I soon began to gasp as I pushed him away.

"Wait...Wait," I whispered. "I'm about to come, but I want to come with you inside me," I said with a sexy grin.

Tony immediately pulled off his underwear. I did the same. I rolled over to my night stand and pulled open my drawer to reveal an assortment of condoms and a bottle of lubrication. Tony just laid there and stroked his dick. I rolled halfway off the bed to get my almost empty bottle of lube. I usually kept it in the drawer with the new bottle, but my fantasy nights with visions of William usually left me too tired to put it back in the drawer. As I reached for the lube my ass was an open target. Tony reached out and lightly caressed it with his finger tips. I froze as I enjoyed his touch. Tony then firmly grabbed my hand and pulled me back on to the bed. He once more tongued me down and maneuvered himself above me. He pinched and licked my nipples as he spread my legs apart with his own leg. He stopped briefly to roll on the condom and lubricate his dick. He squeezed a small amount onto the tips of his fingers and prepared me for his entry. I closed my eyes, clenched my teeth, and moaned with the slight pain that I felt. Fingers never feel like the real thing. Maxwell's sexy voice filled the room as the stereo blared. Tony bent over to kiss me as he slid in. I grunted with pain as it slowly turned into pleasure.

"Wait…Wait!," I grunted.

"I won't hurt you baby. Whenever you ready," Tony whispered as he again licked my ear lobes, my neck, then my nipples. Now relaxed, I reached out to grab his ass to pull him deeper inside me. Slowly, he slid in. As Maxwell's voice filled the room, so did my moans of passion. Tony slid in and out slowly and smoothly. It was like a sexual dance. It wasn't fucking. It wasn't making love. It wasn't even sexing. Tony flowed like a professional, if there is such a thing. He was talented. It was…grooving. Yes, that's what it was. He was grooving me. Soon, he began to take long, slow strokes; almost pulling completely out before going back in deeper. I felt him get harder with every stroke. Unable to control himself, his slow strokes sped up. Before long, he was fucking the hell out of my ass. His grooving turned into heightened, passionate fucking.

"Yeah, baby, take that dick . Come on Craig, take it baby."

"Yeah, Tony, Yeah…." I mumbled as my groans and moans began to turn into dirty talk. Suddenly, Tony's dick exploded into the condom. I felt every twitch as it shot load after load. Lauryn Hill's voice began to sang about the sweetest thing. If she only knew.

Downstairs, William got up and cleaned himself off. He took a long, hot shower. As he stood there, the warm water caressed his body. He thought about everything that had happened. Then, his heart began to feel Craig's pain.

"Damn man, I didn't mean to hurt you. Fuck that bitch. She don't know shit," he thought to himself. He turned off the water and dried himself off. He turned on his CD player. The smooth sexy voice of Luther Vandross filled his apartment. "Endless Love" flowed through William's body as he laid across his bed in only a towel. He drifted off to sleep. What seemed like hours, was merely minutes. In a state of mid sleep, he was suddenly awakened by knocking on his door. He got up and quickly went to the door. But on his way, he realized the knocking was coming from the direction of his room. The knocking was somewhat muffled, but was steady. It stopped, but for only a second or two, like microwaved popcorn when the last few kernels are popping. Then, it started steady again. William walked over to his wall and pressed his ear against it.

"Yeah…baby, yeah…that's it…Yeah, been a long time, huh? Yeah baby, take that shit…Yeah, Craig, take that shit," said one voice.

"Yeah…yeah..Tony, yeah. Shit…Shit!"
William jerked his head away from the wall and slumped back. He stood there, heart racing, eyes wide with amazement and confusion. He went to his bed, sat down, and just stared at the wall. He could not believe his ears. But why should it matter? Was his feelings getting involved? Who was this Tony person, fucking the hell out of Craig? His mind turned as he sat there.

10

We laid there in the after glow in complete silence as the CD had reached the last song and was spinning to the next CD in the disc changer. I knew the routine. Tony would get up, take a shower and have to rush home; 'early day tomorrow,' would be his excuse. He would say that he would call, but wouldn't. I would call him. We would talk about two minutes. Then, he would end the conversation with a story about some boy that he has fallen madly in love with and would ask me not to call anymore. Out of respect, you know. But, hell, it had been a long time and I needed some. I had been through it, so I didn't expect anything more. That's how you play the game. You learn the rules and know what to expect. No one gets hurt. But, something was different this time. Tony just laid there. He laid there a little too long as he looked at the ceiling. Then out of nowhere he asked a question that almost made me choke.

"Who is William?" My heart stopped. I swallowed hard as I tried to speak. But nothing came out. I could not and would not look at Tony because I knew that I would turn into stone or a pillar of salt. So I layed there and just stared at the ceiling as I clutched the sheets close to my chest.

"What...what...do you mean? William?...William who?" I stammered.

"WILLIAM! I said 'William'...You heard me. William! Who is William?" he repeated with frustration.

"What in the fuck are you talking about Tony? William...William is my neighbor from down stairs."

"Hell, he must be getting some of your shit, because you called HIS name out while we were fucking." Tony just got out of bed, shook his head with jealousy, and got dressed. No shower. No small talk. He put on his boots and was out with a bang as he slammed the door. I just laid there staring at the ceiling.

******

William heard what he assumed was Craig's door
slamming. He would not miss the chance to see who it was
making Craig moan and groan like that. He just had to see
who this "Tony" person was. He stood up from his bed and
ran down his short hallway to the kitchen. He ran to the
kitchen sink and looked through the blinds. No one yet. Then,
he saw a shadow approaching. Out of the darkness of night
appeared a man. William could not make out any
distinguishing features. The figure was, however, approaching
an overhead light. William's heart beat faster with jealousy,
anger, and anxiety to see who this person was. The figure was
a few feet away from the light. William leaned closer into the
window. He still could not make out the figure. Suddenly,
William leaped away from the window, backed into his
refrigerator as if some supernatural force had knocked him
away! Was that really him? He knew that it was. The light
shone right on him. William leaned against his refrigerator,
eyes racing in a mad frenzy. All that escaped his lips
was...."Uncle Wes?"

11

William stood there, heart beating a mile a minute. Fear, anger, sadness, amazement, and raw hatred entered his emotional system. There, walking in the darkness of night was William's Uncle Wes. But he had heard Craig's moans of desire saying 'Tony' not 'Wes'. Then, it hit him. Once, while he was out with his uncle, some flaming, obviously gay guy made a terrible mistake and called him Tony in front of William. He had recalled being confused back then, too. He was even more amazed with what his uncle did. He grabbed the guy by the neck and from what William could hear, told him never to call him that name when he was with his family. The guy got the point, because he was almost in tears as he agreed to never let it happen again and shuffled away. William thought about questioning his uncle about it, but decided to let it pass. If he did that to the guy, what would he do to William?

"Tony....Tony....Tony..." William said to himself. It must be some kind of alias, his 'other' name.

What was happening? William felt his life was taking him on a roller coaster ride that he wasn't ready for. He began to shake with fear and anger.

"No!! This shit ain't happening!!" he said as he pushed away from the refrigerator and walked towards his bedroom.

12

"Oh shit, oh shit…" I thought to myself. Had I actually said William's name during sex with Tony? How else would Tony know about him? I got up from my bed and stopped the CD player. It had switched to Heather Headly. I no longer felt lyrically turned on. I clicked on the television instead as I sat there recounting the whole event. No matter how hard I tried, I just could not remember calling out William's name. The sex with Tony was so good, so why was William on my mind? It was almost mystical. It was as if I felt I knew that I had not called out William's name, but my mind was so consumed with William, that Tony had read my mind and saw my deepest thoughts. Yet, I knew that was impossible. I turned it over and over in my head and finally decided to just let it go. "Shit, if I said it, I said it! So what?!" I sat on the bed and looked at the phone. Anger suddenly entered my heart as I began to think about the whole other situation with William.

"Wait a minute! That bitch didn't know me. How in the hell is she gonna say some shit like that?" Then my mind really went into action. I had never met her before. How could she call me out like that? How did she know what was going on? Why was I "the faggot" when both me and William stood there in an embrace? Shit, how did she know that I lived upstairs? She distinctively said "the faggot from upstairs." Unless…unless….

My blood immediately began to bubble. I snatched up the phone and pressed the speed dial button and the number three. Yes, William was already on speed dial, after voicemail on one and Mom and Dad on two. In mid dial, my rational thought stopped me in my tracks. I needed to calm down, first. With one ring, I immediately hung up.

William sat on his bed in a state of confused anger, his phone rang. It only rang once. It was strange, almost a half ring. It really didn't get his attention. He had other issues to consider. He sat there staring into space. His mind again went back…….

✶✶✶✶✶✶

"When is your Mama comin' home, William?"

"She…um…she called and said that she was on her way."

"What happened the other day? You know, with us?"

"What…what are you talking about Uncle Wes?"

"Um..huh..Come here."

"Ma said she was on her way," lied William.

"I know how long it takes your mama to get home, boy. Come here and give your uncle a hug." William slowly got up from the table and walked over to his Uncle who was sitting on the couch in the living room. He went over and stood directly in front of him, head bowed in fear, embarrassment, and shame. Wes looked up at him for a few seconds and sighed. The only other sound that you heard was the ticking of the grandfather clock that stood in the corner. "Tick…tick…tick…" Slowly, his uncle stood up. Now he was directly standing in front of William, William felt his warmth. The familiar scent of Irish Spring soap played with William's nostrils. As his Uncle stood up, something protruded from his crotch area. He was aroused. It was just inches away from William's hip.

"Go ahead, touch it," he said in a low sexy voice. "You know what to do." William's heart raced and his palms began to sweat. He slowly raised his right hand to touch his uncle. He closed his eyes as his hand made contact with his uncle's aroused penis. His uncle let out a moan as he too closed his eyes and tilted his head back. He reached out both hands and placed each one on William's shoulders as he savored the familiar touch of his nephew's hands.

"Yeah boy, rub it. Rub it," he gasped as he began to move his hips. William's eyes were clamped shut as he tried to take himself away. His uncle couldn't take it any longer. He grabbed William's shoulders and pulled him closer to him. Now their bodies meshed together. Once again, William began to get aroused. With all of his might, he tried to make it stop, but his own penis twitched as his uncle moved himself against him. They stood there grinding for a few minutes. They stood there in what appeared to be an embrace as William's mother walked in.

40

"Wha…what's wrong…what…what happened? William you alright?" she stammered. Uncle Wes held William against him. He would not let his sister see his erection. William's heart almost stopped as he realized his mother had just walked in. Luckily, his back was to her or she would have seen the raw fear in his eyes.

"He's okay, just something he needed to talk to his uncle about," Wes said as he winked at William's mother, indicating to her that everything was okay. "He's alright, Harriet. Now go on in the kitchen, the boy ain't want you seeing him cry."

"You alright, William?" she asked with complete concern, not fully understanding the situation. After a few seconds of silence, and a pinch from his uncle, William responded.

"Yeah…um..yeah, Ma, I'm alright."

"Leave the boy alone Harriet," said Wes.

"We'll talk about it later if you want to, baby." Still with a confused and concerned look on her face, she disappeared into the kitchen. His uncle then released him from their embrace, reached into his pants to adjust himself and sat down on the couch.

"Go on, boy," he said not even looking at William, as he flipped through the channels. William, still slightly erect turned to walk away. Suddenly…..DING! DING! DING! The clock rang and scared the hell out of him.

William realized that it was his phone that was ringing and not the clock from his memory. Finally on the fifth ring, he picked it up.

"Hello?"

"William, its me Craig, we need to talk."

"Oh….I guess we do….so talk," William said matter-of-factly. I sensed coldness in his voice. It almost scared me. How could he be bitter when I was the one who got verbally attacked by his little girlfriend?

"William, what's up with you? Why are you acting like this?"

"Like what, Craig? You called me to talk. So talk." I didn't like it, but I was still mad about Cicely. I swallowed the pill that William was giving me and decided to go with my original purpose of the call.

41

"William, something is not sitting well with me. Now, I don't know who she is or what she is to you, but she had no right saying to me what she said."

"You're right, Craig, and I apologize," William said dryly.

"And just what are you apologizing for, William?"

"I'm just saying I'm sorry she called you that name. That's what I'm apologizing for."

"Wait a minute, William. All she saw was you and me hugging. How is she going to call me the faggot and not you?"

"How do you know that she didn't? You weren't here all night," he flatly responded.

"I might as well have been. I heard everything," I thought. But William's question threw a wrench in my plan. So I went to plan B.

"Um...now, more importantly, how in the hell did she know that I lived upstairs? She said 'the faggot from UPSTAIRS' didn't she?" There was that brief moment of silence as I waited for William's answer. Although I was upset, I was glowing because I just knew I had William pinned against the wall with that question. Then, William spoke.

"Check this out Craig. I've got a better question for you. ...Who in the fuck is Tony?" And with those words, my heart stopped as the phone fell out of my hands. William heard the phone fall, but sat in silence waiting for my answer.

"Who? What did you say?"

"Who is Tony?"

"Tony who? What...what are you talking about, William?

"Who just left your apartment, Craig?"

"What!? What's up with you, William? You watching me now? You watching who comes in and out of my apartment? So I guess you are, huh? You saw him leave? Yeah, Tony just left. You know Tony?"

"Look, Craig, how do you know Tony?"

"What?!!!! How in the fuck you gonna ask me some shit like that? What does the answer to that question have to do with you?"

"It has everything to do with me..Every thing! How do you know Tony?!"

"Look William, you need to calm down and let it go. Do you know Tony? Huh? Is he one of your boys? What is it William? Is it hard for you to find out that one of your boys gets down with other guys? Huh, William? Huh?" I teased. And once again, there was that long dramatic pause. All that you heard was breathing. And out of the silence came William's shaky voice.

"He's my fucking uncle, Craig. That's who he is." And with those words, I was left with a dial tone. My ear was glued to the phone. Although I knew William had hung up, I could not let go of the receiver. Had I heard him correctly? Did he just say that Tony was his uncle? Wait a minute. Tony was his name, not Wes. I was finally able to hang up the phone. I stood up and began to pace my apartment rubbing my temples. This was too much for me. I needed to get out. I yanked open all of my drawers and pulled out some fleece pants and an old college sweatshirt. Where I was going, I didn't know. I just knew that I needed some air. I tied my shoe laces and grabbed my key, and with a loud slam, I was out.

William, sitting in a state of anger, guilt, and fear, heard what he knew was Craig's door slamming again. "Oh, no…Oh shit, I know he ain't coming down here to start no shit. I can't look at him right now," William said as he got up to go to his door to wait for Craig's knock. One minute passed. Two passed. There was no knocking on his door. Suddenly, he heard an engine turning. He then made his way to the kitchen window where he saw headlights casting shadows into his apartment. As he looked through his blinds, he saw Craig's tail lights and heard his tires screeching as he left the parking lot like a bat out of hell.

"Oh shit…That nigga better not be headed to see my uncle!" William said to himself as he ran to put on some clothes. He rushed into his room and jumped into the first pair of pants and shirt he saw. In a matter of minutes, he was sitting in his black Navigator and leaving the complex. He made his way around each curve until he was at the gate.

"Damn…where did he go?" Craig's car was no where in sight. The gate must have been open already, because William's lights were the only ones in the area. There were two ways to go and William chose the route that Craig didn't take. He realized this as he traveled and did not see his car.

"He must have took the other way….Shit, it doesn't matter, I will still beat him there, if I go this way," he said as he hung a right at the end of the street.

My heart raced as I listened to Brandy's "Never Say Never." I had no clue where I was going. Trees were a blur as I sped down the desolate back road. I could not believe where this fantasy was taking me. I never knew that I had to unleash skeletons, monsters, and devils from my closet just to experience this fantasy.

"It's not worth it! It's just not worth it, God," I said to myself. "What am I doing wrong? What in the hell am I doing wrong?!" I could not believe that I was yelling at the top of my lungs in my car. When I realized that I was yelling, I began to laugh at myself. "Craig, come on, man, what are you doing to yourself? Just leave William the fuck alone, and leave Tony or Wes, or whatever his fuckin' name might be, alone, too. It's just that simple," I told myself. This seemed to calm me down just a little. I slowed down as Brandy told me that almost doesn't count. "You right, Brandy, almost doesn't count. It's all or nothing….All or nothing, baby."

13

"Damn, where is he," William asked himself as he pulled onto the street just a few houses down from his uncle's house. The street was quiet and dark. It was a little after 4 A.M. He did not see Craig's car. He did, however, see his uncle's car and another car right behind it that he did not recognize. William hated coming on this side of town every since his mother told him that his uncle Wes was moving in the area. He knew where he lived, but Wes had no clue that William lived in the same subdivision as Craig. Just as he was about to pull away, headlights appeared in the distance. "Maybe that's him," William thought to himself. He sat and waited as the car got closer and closer. It wasn't Craig, but it slowed down as it approached his uncle's house. The car parked on the side street opposite the house. Three of the four doors of the car opened. Out of the car emerged three tall, muscular men. They all had cups in their hands that apparently carried alcohol. They all stumbled and laughed as they held on to each other trying to maintain their balance. They finally made their way to the door. All of the lights appeared to be off in the house, but some type of lighting was dimly lighting each room. The group stood in front of the door for a minute or two. Finally, someone answered the door. He looked like he could have been his uncle Wes, but it was too dark to be sure. The three men stood at the door talking to the guy who opened the door. They laughed and joked for a minute or two. Soon, the group entered and closed the door behind them. What was going on? William decided to wait a little longer. He would not let Craig cause any more drama than what had already brewed. He was prepared to stop him at any cost.

As he waited, he began to dose off as rain began to drizzle on his windows. Just as he nodded off for the second time, a car pulled up behind him. An apparently intoxicated man who was obviously in his early forties, but had a body of a race horse, got out of the car. He stumbled past William's truck and noticed this beautiful man dozing off. William was awakened by someone knocking on his window. The rain had slowed to a very light drizzle.

"Hey…..Hey…You comin' in to the party?" asked the strange man.

"Um….yeah….yeah, I was just..um.. waitin' for my boy to show up," lied William.

"You must have been waitin a long time. You was knocked out, man. Come on in with me. I don't think your boy is gonna show up. It's gettin' late and the party just kicking off." William looked at the man and then towards his uncle's house. He thought for a minute and finally pulled his keys from the ignition as he prepared to get out. "What kind of party is just kicking off at 4:00 a.m.," thought William.

"Aite, man, but whose party is this?"

"Shit, Hell if I know," laughed the man. "I heard about it from some friend of mine. I think the guy's name is Tony. He has these parties all the time. This one was a last minute thing, though."

The guy reached out to shake William's hand and introduced himself. The two men walked toward the house. William looked over his shoulders to see if Craig was anywhere in sight. Soon, they were at the door. William could here some music. Now, close enough to the house to see, he noticed that it was lit by candle light and a few lamps. The guy knocked on the door. For a minute or two, no one showed up. Then, the door slowly began to open. A slim, model looking guy stuck his head out of the door. He looked the guy up and down. Then he looked William up and down.

"Aite, aite, looks good. Y'all tight….come on in," he said. He then stood aside and opened the door all the way. William was confused. He saw clothes, towels, and heard strange noises in between the beats of the music. Then, he saw some dude walk by in a towel and some Timberland boots. The guy paused for a minute as he scanned William from head to toe. William ignored the guy and just scanned the room. Although he was confused, he was torn. He just couldn't walk away. He began to walk deeper into the house. He was in such a trance, that he did not hear the guy telling him that he needed to leave his clothes in a bag on the couch. In one swift step, he soon realized he was in over his head. In the one room he decided to walk in, the scene was too much. Trying to catch his breath, he looked to the left---SEX! He looked to the right---SEX! On the floor---SEX! On one of the make-shift beds---SEX! Not men and women, but MEN!! Men were sucking each other's dicks. They were sticking their fingers in other men's asses. And two men were actually having intercourse. One guy was really fucking another guy in the ass! William immediately broke out! He turned for the door and pushed one guy down as he reached for the door knob. In seconds, he was gone.

"Who in the hell was that?" asked Wes as he emerged from the kitchen in a towel. He then went to his window and saw a Navigator screeching down his street. He just stared out of the window for a minute or two and shook his head, then went back into one of the rooms to enjoy his guests.

"Oh shit, Oh shit, oh shit!!! Hell no! Hell, fuckin' no! What in the fuck was that? What in the fuck is goin on?!!!!" William yelled as he floored it down the back roads of the neighborhood. He couldn't believe what he had just witnessed. Men, yes men were having sex at his uncle's house. It was some type of orgy. He just couldn't believe it. The images of the men could not leave his head. He finally made it back to his apartment, and decided to call it a night or more like morning since it was almost 5 a.m. He parked his truck and made his way to his door. He just shook his head and said to himself, "Man! What a fucking night!" But it was just the beginning. William froze. He found me drunk and in tears, on his door step.

"I need you William," I cried. "I need you William. I don't know what the fuck to do, William. I need you, man." William stood there for a minute or two.

"Get up, Craig," he said as he reached out his hand. I took his hand and clumsily stood on my feet. I wrapped my arms around him and cried into his shoulders. William reached into his pockets and pulled out his keys. As he held me with one hand, he unlocked his door with the other hand.

"Come on, man," William said as he led me into his apartment. I continued mumbling words and phrases. William just held on to me tightly as he led me deeper into the apartment. He closed the door behind us. He closed door 655. He turned the lock and made sure the door was closed this time. He held me in an embrace and just shook his head. "I need you, too Craig. I need you, too. I need to understand this shit!"

PART II

14

William led me back to his bedroom. I continued to cry and mumble as I laid on his shoulder.

"Come on man, Come on Craig, its alright man. Come on!" William said as he opened his bedroom door to carry me in. He laid me across the bed. I continued to mumble and sob. William untied my shoes and pulled each one off. I was jelly in his hands. He started to unbutton my shirt. Suddenly, I jerked up, with tears in my eyes.

"I'm sorry William. I'm so fucking sorry William. I need you. I need to talk to you William.."

"Come on Craig. Relax," he said as he gently pushed me back down. He then unzipped my pants and pulled them down. He didn't realize that my body was just as nice as his; smaller, but just as nice. He paused for a moment. He shook his head when he realized that he was standing there admiring another man's body. His heart began to beat faster as the view of my body took his mind back to the orgy scene that he had just experienced.

"What the fuck is wrong with me?" he questioned as he covered me with a blanket and turned to walk away. He began to close his door, but stopped and took one last look at me laying there in his bed.

"Why do you need me, Craig?" he asked himself as he closed the door. He walked out into the living room. He sat down on his couch and took off his shoes. He made himself comfortable as he reached for the blanket at the end of the couch. He clicked on the television. In a matter of minutes he was asleep.

15

How I knew where William's bathroom was, I did not know. I just knew that I had to piss. I stood there in front of the toilet and just let it flow. Finishing up, I washed my hands and flipped the light off. I decided to see if William was awake. I opened the bedroom door and made my way down the hall. There was William, sprawled across the couch. One of his legs was drooped over the edge. The sheet was at his waist and covered him to his ankles. He had taken off his shirt and I stood there looking over him admiring each and every cut of his chiseled chest. The only light in the room came from the television, casting shadows throughout the room. I tip-toed over to turn it off.

"Don't do that," said William, causing me to freeze. "I'm watchin' that," he said in a sexy baritone voice.

"Oh, I'm sorry, William.. I thought you were asleep."

"Nope, I'm wide awake. And look!" he said as he dramatically threw the sheet off to reveal that he was butt ass naked. His dick was hard as a steel pole and pointed straight up.

"Yep, I'm wide awake, and…and…so is he," he said as he licked his lips, looked down towards his dick, and then looked me dead in my eyes. I could not believe this was happening. My heart began to beat uncontrollably, my mouth got dry, and my own dick began to grow.

"Come here, Craig," William said as he began to stroke his dick. "I'm not what you need. This is what you need, Craig. Come on, man. It will be our little secret. Come here, baby. You know you want this."

I could not control myself. I immediately walked over to the couch and knelt between it and the coffee table. I put my hand over William's and began to help him stroke that huge dick. Then with my other hand, I cupped his balls and rubbed his slightly hairy inner thighs. William opened his legs wider to feel the complete sensation of my warm hands. Soon he began to grind his hips into my hand. I couldn't hold back any longer. I had to get a taste. I leaned closer to William's body and slowly opened my mouth. The manly scent of William's crotch teased my nostrils. I opened my mouth wide as the head of William's dick brushed past my lips and

49

touched the roof of my mouth. William let out a moan as he grabbed my head and forced himself down my throat.

"Yeah, Craig, suck it, baby. Suck that dick, nigga." I began to hungrily slurp William's dick. He began to moan and groan as he ran his hands over my head, neck, and ears. William's moans and touch made me wild with desire to have him inside me. Then, in one quick movement, William grabbed my head and just said, "Stop! I want to fuck you...."

My eyes widened as I looked into William's eyes and then back at his dick.

"Come on, you know you want to. Come on Craig." I stood up and removed my boxer briefs. I then put one foot up on the couch between William's thigh and the couch. I kept the other foot on the floor. William reached over and held my waist on both sides. I grabbed William's dick and slowly guided it into my ass. I slowly slid down on it with an ease that made William call out the Lord's name in vain.

"Ride this dick, Craig. Ride this shit, yo," William growled. I soon began to bounce up and down on William's dick.

"Yeah, take that dick, boy take that dick. That's some good ass!. Damn, nigga. That shit is better than my girl's shit. Take it Craig. Damn, that shit is tight!" I still couldn't believe that this was actually happening. It was all too much. I closed my eyes to enjoy the ride. I moaned with pleasure as I thought of all the many nights when I dreamed of this night. I wanted to cry. But, I wanted to look into William's eyes to see how much pleasure he was experiencing. I rolled my head back up to face William. I slowly opened my eyes. There, below me was no longer William. It was a stranger's face. Yet, it was strangely familiar. I couldn't believe my eyes.

"Yeah Craig ride this dick. Ride it baby!!"

"Noooooooooo!" I yelled as I sat straight up and realized that I was still in William's bed. My chest pounded as I tried to catch my breath.

"It was a fuckin' dream! Thank God," I said rubbing my temples. It was so real, though. But whose face did I see? I then noticed that I was almost naked. "What is going on? What did I do last night? Damn, my head is killing me," I said as I pulled the covers away. I had a hangover from hell. I couldn't remember anything from last night. Then, I wondered where William was. I stood up, went to the door, and slowly opened it. I could hear the static of the television. William was still asleep. There he was, sprawled across the couch. And there IT was, wishing me a 'good morning'. William's dick was standing straight up under the thin sheet that barely covered his waist. I paused for a minute or two, savoring the view, yet thinking how ironic it was. Could my dream be materializing? I was too scared to move towards the television. So, I stood there. But soon, my own dick began to grow. I slowly reached down to grab it. I was actually getting turned on by staring at the print of William's dick against the sheet. I began to stroke my dick as I stood there admiring William's erection. All I thought about was the smell, the taste, the feel of that hot dick from my dream. I stood there in the shadows, jacking off. With my other hand, I began pinching and rubbing my nipples. William could wake up at any minute, but I was too close. I was on the edge of shooting. The idea of William catching me doing this made it all the more pleasurable. And soon, I was there.

"Oh shit, oh shit," I whispered. And in a matter of minutes, I was spewing my fluids all over my hands and underwear. Finally catching my breath, I stood there for a few seconds, staring at William's erection. "Damn, that was good William," I whispered. Now, I needed a shower. I headed to William's bathroom.

William rolled over on his side and opened one eye. Craig had walked away. He then rolled back over to face the television screen. He smiled to himself, closed his eyes, and went back to sleep.

I stumbled back to the bedroom, holding my dick until I could get it all cleaned up. I took a long hot shower. "Damn, that felt good," I said as I dried off. I wrapped the towel around my waist and stepped into the bedroom. I walked over and sat on William's bed. My headache was still there, but not as intense as before. Then, slowly, it hit me. All of the events of last night began to come back in bits and pieces. I had forgotten about it all. But now, now I remembered who the stranger was that I saw in the dream....

LAST NIGHT

16

After finding out that Tony was William's Uncle Wes, it was too much for me to digest. I needed to get out. I drove aimlessly for quite sometime, but driving through the city usually presented me with something, or somebody, to do. I still couldn't get William off my mind.

"What is it?! Why did you put this man into my life, God? Why? You must got somethin really good planned for me." I continued to drive aimlessly. Brandy's raspy, yet mellow voice blared through my speakers, calming my nerves. Lights, buildings, even people were a blur to me as my heart and mind battled with each other. But suddenly, my eyes gained focus. As I slowed down, I saw the sign clearly. I didn't realize that I was in this particular area, but here was the sign. "CYPRESS STREET" Now, I had been down this street many times, but not at this hour. I made the right turn on to the street. I couldn't believe I was actually there. There was no harm in checking out the 'Hoe Stroll' as the locals called it. As soon as I turned onto the street, I spotted three other sets of headlights coming my way. The first two cars sped by. However, the last car slowed down. As it approached my car, I slowed down. The car got closer and closer. My heart pounded. I had never done anything like this before. Well, I had looked at guys at intersections and grocery stores, but never in a situation where I absolutely knew what was going on. As the car slowly passed me, I got the disappointment of a lifetime. There, just feet away from me was a big gray-haired-- make that *white*-haired, white guy. It wasn't so much that he was white, but the man appeared to be in his late 60's. I sped on by and laughed to myself. I needed that laugh. I decided to circle around one last time and call it a night. I would get some sleep, relax, and talk to William about everything tomorrow. As I drove up to the next cross street, an image emerged from the darkness. It was almost as if it was a shadow or a ghost and not an actual human.

The figure stood against one of the buildings across the street. As I got closer, my head lights shone on the lower part of the shadow's body. Boots; tan, Timberlands, sloppily laced.. Jeans; oversized, sagging and bunched up at the top of the boots. Boxers; navy blue plaid. Shirt; baby blue, sleeves ripped off, hands stuffed in the pockets with a black backpack on one shoulder. He had one foot propped against the building. That was all that I saw as I drove by. I continued driving, but decided to turn around to get one last view. I stopped at the end of the strip and made a U-turn. I slowly approached the building where the guy stood. This time, my view was quite clear and crisp. The image, now a real human being, was a light skinned guy with a small afro. As I pulled closer, the guy licked his thin upper lip, then lightly sucked on his drooping bottom lip. I stopped at the intersection and made eye contact with the stranger. He looked at me and shrugged his shoulders with his hands out as if to say, "So, whassup?" I pulled over and turned off the engine. The stranger looked to the left and then he looked to the right before making a move. He loosened up and pushed himself away from the wall. He was on his way to my car. His boots dragged as his bowlegged walk made me smile. There is just something about bowlegged boys that make me weak. The stranger leaned down onto my window.

"What da deal, yo?" he said. Then, out of nowhere, he smiled. The stranger licked his lips and smiled at me.

"What's so funny?" I asked..

"You, nigga. Check you out. You mad cute. You got a nice ride. You got all yo teeth and shit. What a nigga like you doin' on da strip?" he asked as he comfortably got closer to me. This would have normally made me uncomfortable, but I was cool. I was actually enjoying the guy's company. His breath was fresh and warm. I smiled and decided to ignore his question.

"So how old are you?" I asked.

"Old enough to look yo ass in the eye and say you need to get the hell off dis strip and go home!" he said with a sexy grin.

"Whatever, man.." I said. Just then, it started to drizzle. "So you getting in or what?"
The guy looked around and looked up into the sky.

"Shit!' he said as he made his way around to the passenger side. He jumped in and made himself comfortable. I didn't know what to say at this point. Soon, the stranger began to talk, as he tossed his backpack in the back seat.

"Yo, on the real, what a nigga like you doin out this late and in this area?"

"Just a lot of shit goin on. Just kind of ended up here," I said with a shrug.

"Me too."

"Say, what," I asked.

"Nothin, yo…So…um…Where we goin?"

"I don't know, man, you tell me," I said.

"Aite, drive up this street, turn right and just keep goin," the stranger said. I followed directions and started driving. The rain really started to pour down as Denise William's , "Silly," began to play on the radio. I reached to change it, thinking that this thug would think I was a punk for liking this song. But before I reached the button, he grabbed my hand.

"Leave it yo." And so I did.

"The name is Silas, but people call me Red….. Yo! Turn right here! Park ovah there." I parked the car in a secluded lot as Denise Williams kept pleading for love to stop making a fool of her. Her voice floated through the car as the rain drops tattered on the roof and windshield. Then out of nowhere, Silas turned to me and asked:

"You evah made love in the rain, yo?" I almost choked. I began to cough uncontrollably.

"I can't say that I have, man," I finally responded.

"Come on!" Silas said as he jumped out of the car into the pouring rain. He ran and sat on the hood and just stared into the sky as the rain poured all over his light, smooth face. I sat in the car, still in awe. I was not about to have sex with some stranger that I just met off the street. But the kid was fine, though. And there he was sitting on the hood of my car, looking into the sky like he was some witch doctor or something waiting for a sign from the heavens. The boy had it going on. His toned, tight arms revealed tender muscles with strong protruding veins. Then, with rain pouring down his face and a drenched baby blue shirt, he turned to look me dead in the eyes. And with those two beautiful pink lips, he spat some excess water to the side of the car then mouthed to me,

"Come on!" And it was as if I was hypnotized. My legs, my hands, my entire body began to move on their own accord. Before I knew it, I was standing in the pouring rain staring at Silas. He reached out and put his hands on my hips. For that one moment in time, I felt the strangest feeling. It was a mixture of love, lust, passion, desire, fear, and confusion all bottled up. But before I could separate all of these emotions, my lips were being devoured by Silas'. The rain poured between our faces and ran down our necks. Silas pulled me closer so that I was lodged between his legs as he sat on the hood of the car. He then slid off the hood, colliding into my wet body with a loud SMACK. I could feel his rock hard manhood as it pressed through his soaking wet jeans. The complete wetness of our clothing pressing against each other was raunchy and sensual. My hands slid up and down his wet, muscular arms as I tried to feel every wet part of him. He suddenly ripped away his shirt and then grabbed mine. I was so lost in emotion that I let him lead the way. Soon we were both chest to chest. The rain poured down our backs as our tongues probed deep into each others throats. I began to moan and hump up against his rigid dick. It was a dirty feeling that felt so sexy and sensual at the same time.

"Yeah, kid...This is the shit, right!" Silas moaned into my ear as he then licked every inch of it, inside and out. I could not respond, because he had already reached and grabbed my ass with one hand and my dick with the other. I was in ecstasy. Before I knew it, my pants began to fall. I snapped back to reality and grabbed my pants. Silas roughly pushed my hands away. "No, it's aite, man. Ain't nobody around. Come on....come on."

The rain had drenched my boxer briefs as I let him take control. They stuck to every rigid curve of my ass and my now hard dick. Silas then unzipped his pants and let them fall to his ankles too. He turned me around and pulled my round, hot ass closer to his dick. My ass merged with his body with another wet 'SMACK!' Silas began to bite and lick my neck as he humped my wet ass. The rain poured down our bodies. Not a soul was in sight in the secluded lot. With my back turned, enjoying the hot moment, I didn't see Silas reaching down for a condom in his pocket. He pulled down his boxers and rolled on the condom in two swift moves. He continued to kiss and bite my neck. He then tugged at my underwear. "No, Silas. I can't," I protested.

"Come on. I got you baby. I just want to feel your skin on my skin, baby."

My underwear slowly slid down. I could not believe this was happening. I couldn't believe that I was letting this happen. I just thought to myself, "What the hell?" I then thought I felt Silas' dick rubbing against my ass cheeks. Then, all of a sudden, before I could really process the thought, I felt this unbearable pain! Silas had permeated my entire soul with his rock hard dick.

"I got you baby...I got you...Just hold on...Hold on..." he said as he held me tightly. It hurt so badly. I let two tears roll down my cheek as I gritted my teeth to bear the pain and try to push him away. He held on tightly and slowly began to pump in and out of my ass. The pain slowly subsided and pleasure began to take over. I couldn't believe it. I was having sex with a fucking stranger in the fucking rain. Our bodies began to smack into each other with loud, wet claps. It was so hot. Silas went hard, hard and fast. He grunted with each thrust. Our bodies slipped and slid against each other. Silas was getting close.

"I'm about to nut, yo...I'm about to nut!" And with those words, he pulled out, ripped off the condom, and hot shots of cum spattered all over my wet ass. Although the rain was cool, I could feel the warm streams landing on my ass. Silas jerked and jerked until he had every drop out. I had already come minutes before he did. We just stood there holding each other as the rain poured on our bodies. Me, against the hood with my back towards him and Silas pressed close against my back, breathing on my neck.

I now tried to remember what caused me to go drink so much. Was that all we did? The sex was off the hook. It wasn't that. I then recalled getting angry about something. I sat there on the edge of William's bed as tears began to roll down my face. It hit me like a brick. The tears poured and poured. My whole body began to shake because I remembered......

17

As Silas and I sat in the car in wet clothes and some towels that I had in my trunk, the radio talked of light rain in the area. The two of us sat in silence. We were driving through the city, still a little distance from my place, but not too far from where Silas lived. I was smiling ear to ear with a glow. It was just what I needed to take my mind off of William. However, nothing could prepare me for what happened next. Silas bit his bottom lip as he kept looking over at me, then back at the road. He looked one last time at the road, then at me.

"Yo, I got somethin' to tell you, man."

"What's up, Red? Yeah, I'm gonna call you Red now. Wait, don't tell me. You straight right?" I laughed. He didn't.

"I'm positive, yo." It really didn't register with me. I kept driving. "Say what, Red?"

"I'm....positive."

"You positive about what?"

"No, nigga, I'm positive. You know HIV positive." I drove for a few seconds then immediately screeched on the brakes!

"What?!! Get out!!!! Get the fuck out, you dirty motherfuckin punk! Get the fuck out!"

"I wore a condom!" I reached under my seat and pointed a gun at him.

"GET OUT! I said with the look of Satan in my eyes. Silas quickly unlocked the door and jumped out, leaving his back pack in my back seat. I sped off, leaving him standing in the rain in the middle of nowhere. The rain pouring on his face blended with the one tear that fell from his eyes as he watched me speed off.

I sat on the edge of the bed. "He was HIV positive," I whispered to myself, over and over again. "....and I let him fuck me...."

"Hey. Wassup, Craig? You up?" said a voice from behind the door. William was knocking. "You alright, man?" I collected myself and quickly wiped my tears away.

"Yeah...ummm, yeah...I'm fine, man," I coughed out. "I'll be out in a minute. What...umm..what are you cooking me for breakfast?" I asked, trying to make light of the situation.

"You just hurry up and get your drunk ass out of my room!" William joked and turned to walk away from the door. But my mind and heart was totally off course and would not allow me to laugh. Did I have A.I.D.S? Would I get sick? Would I die? The tears again began to flow.

"Come on Craig, get it together! Just go get tested. Everything will be just fine," I said to myself. I took a deep breath, got up and wrapped a towel around my waist. I went to open the door, making sure my face showed no signs of crying. Maybe William would think that I was still slightly hung over. I slowly walked down the hallway into the kitchen. William had his back turned. He was reaching up in one of the cabinets. He stood there in only some boxers. His calves flexed as he reached for some cereal.

"All I got is cereal, man," he said as he slowly turned around. "Oh...um...I guess you need some clothes," he said with an embarrassed look on his face, realizing I was only wearing a towel..

"That would be a good idea, unless you want me to stroll around here half naked."

"You ain't got nothin I wanna see or haven't seen, Craig."

"Is that so?" I said with a forced grin. "By the way, sorry about everything."
William turned his head to one side and raised his brows, as if to say, "Oh really?"

"Yeah, we'll talk man. Um...I'll get some shorts and a T-shirt for you. There's the cereal, the milk is in the fridge, and here's a bowl. Help yourself. I'm gonna get my shower now," William said as he passed by me. "I'll leave the shorts and shirt out on the bed." And he disappeared down the hall and into his bedroom. I got some milk and poured it over the cereal. I sat down and began to eat. Suddenly, a vision of

Silas flashed through my mind. I dropped the spoon and my appetite was gone.

"How could I be so stupid? What was I thinking?" Soon, I heard the shower running. I figured that the coast was clear for me to check out the clothes that William had laid out for me. I walked down the hallway and into the bedroom. The door was cracked and the steam escaped from the opening. I could really hear the water running now. Another flash of Silas passed across my eyes, his water drenched face looking me in the eyes. I blinked, rubbed my eyes, and shook my head. No matter what I tried, Silas would not flee my mind.

18

Silas stood there in the rain. He saw headlights in the distance, but he didn't care. All he thought about was Craig. He had fucked up again. Honesty had failed him once more. Cars sped by, splashing water on his already soaking wet clothes. But God was looking out for him as the down pour turned into a light drizzle. Although the street was desolate, he realized that he wasn't too far from home. Another set of headlights appeared in the distance behind him. Silas continued walking, oblivious to the fact that the car was slowing down. It pulled up close to him. The window slowly rolled down.

"Hey, I thought that was you. You need a ride?" Silas wiped his face to clear his vision. He crouched down and squinted to see the dark figure behind the wheel.

"Ah man...not you," he said as he straightened up and walked closer to the window.

"At least you can act like you glad to see me. What you doin out here so late, anyway?"

"You know me, the street life is the life I know best," responded Silas.

"Yeah, that's what's gonna get yo ass in trouble," the driver joked. "Anyway, you wanna ride? I got a couple of people coming over to play some cards and shit. I know you ain't too far from home, but I can give you a lift. Look at you, you soaked, man." Silas closed his eyes, took a deep breath and walked across to the passenger side of the car. He opened the door and got in. The car was in motion.

"Why are you so wet? What have you been gettin into tonite?" Silas just closed his eyes and sank deeper into his seat.

19

Visions of Silas left my head long enough for me to put on the clothes that William had left out. I lifted the shorts to see if William had given me a pair of his underwear.

"Damn, I couldn't be so lucky," I thought as I slid into the shorts and pulled the shirt over my head. Soon, I heard the water stop running. I then heard William's baritone voice attempting to sing:

"Love, oh love, stop making a fool of meeeee!" I couldn't control the tears this time. My whole body shook. This was the same song that was playing when I met Silas. The same song that played before me and Silas had sex and I kicked him out of my car. There was no stopping it now. William was on his way out and would see the tears. He hummed as he took one quick glimpse of himself in the mirror. He walked out into his bedroom and found me devastated, tearful, and shaking on the edge of his bed, wearing what I would later find out were his favorite shorts and T-shirt. He didn't know what to say. He didn't know what to do. He stood there for a minute or two just staring at me.

"Craig...what's up, man," he finally questioned. I was so engrossed in my state of sadness that I couldn't speak. William stood there in complete silence; puzzled by the tears, yet concerned with compassion. Seeing another man cry made his heart a little weak. It wasn't a tear or two, it was all out water works with trembling and sniffling. William was torn. He was afraid. His heart said comfort this fellow human being. But his head said remember what happened the last time that you consoled this gay man. Minutes later, the two systems came to a compromise. William walked over and sat on the bed, inches from me, but he would not touch me. I continued crying, but slowly gained control. The trembling subsided, but the tears continued to well up in my eyes.

"I'm sorry William. I didn't mean for you to see...to see me like this," I said sniffling as I spoke.

"It's aite, man. Are you okay?"

"Um...uh..yeah. I'm aite." William had a strange feeling that maybe this had something to do with his Uncle Wes. But he would not bring it up. It wasn't the time for it now. Yet, he couldn't be more wrong.

"William, we really need to talk," I said as I subconsciously rested my hand on his thigh. This caught William off guard.

"I....I....I don't know where to begin, William. You....Us...Your Uncle; Tony or Wes, whatever his name is....It's all...Its just all so fucking crazy!" I continued rambling as William tuned out my voice. He didn't understand why his dick was rising. Before he knew it, I was crying into his shoulder. William slowly lifted his arms and wrapped them around me. The harder I cried, the tighter William held me. I felt William's grip tighten. Comfort and sheer amazement stopped my tears. William was actually holding me. I closed my eyes to savor the moment. The strength, the power, the warmth...those arms could have lulled me to sleep, but they didn't. They ignited a desire. I slowly lifted my head. My ear pushed across William's chin. Still in William's embrace, I raised my head a little more. Cheek to cheek, we sat there in silence. I parted my lips to let the slightest breath escape my mouth and pass across William's cheek. A little higher, I lifted my head. Now, our lips were millimeters from each other. I couldn't resist. I didn't care if William knocked the shit out of me. I was going for it. Our lips touched. The warmth of his lips sent waves through me. William did not move. His eyes were clenched and his lips remained stationary. It was as if I was attempting to give a goodnight kiss to a sleeping relative.

I then opened my mouth and let the tip of my tongue slip out. I tasted every inch of William's lips. The warmth, the smell, the electricity made me dizzy. For an entire minute, I tried to kiss William lightly and cautiously. Yet, William did not respond. Just when I was about to give up, I felt William's embrace tighten, again. My eyes shot wide open in amazement. Still lip to lip, I looked William in the face. His eyes were shut tight. His lips opened and he began to devour mine. His grip around me was so tight that it started to affect my breathing. But I didn't care. William was kissing me back! Finally, getting over the shock, I decided to participate. We both hungrily devoured each other's lips. What was he doing? William was actually kissing another man! He wanted to stop, but he couldn't. He wanted to release his embrace and run into the world, but he couldn't. All that he could do was sit there, hold me, and kiss me!

Catching my breath, I looked into William's face. The tension was still there and his eyes were still tightly closed. His chest heaved in and out as he too tried to catch his breath. He had just kissed another man. A real kiss! Slowly, his eyes opened to see my awe struck face. Yet, he didn't move. He wouldn't. His grasp on me loosened but his arms remained around my body.

"Damn!" I said softly, still attempting to catch my breath. William's tongue had just explored my mouth. And now we sat there looking into each other's eyes. William began to speak, but I put my fingers against his lips and said, "Shhhh!, don't say anything."

I reached around William and slowly laid him back on the bed. And there we laid, in each other's arms.

PART III

20

"It's been a long time, huh, Silas, or should I say 'Red'?" said the driver of the car as they pulled into the parking garage.

"Yeah, its been a minute," Silas responded. He knew what this meant. The driver wanted to come upstairs, not spend the night, just come up and chill for a little while.

"So, what are you doin tomorrow, or should I say today?"

"I don't know, I got an interview with this company down town. You know me; always on the grind."

"Sounds good. So…can I…ahhh…come up, before I head home?" Silas thought deep and hard. What lie to tell this time? Fuck it! He would just tell him, 'NO.'

"Ummm…Nah, not tonite, Wes."

"Hey, that's Tony to you, boy! Why you acting crazy. Don't let that shit slip again," he said aggressively.

"Whateva yo." And he was on his way up to his apartment. Wes' car backed out and disappeared in the distance. He had been turned down by Silas, but he had just had sex with Craig. He would just go home to join his party that had already been set up by one of his boys at his house.

Silas went in and sat on his couch. All that he could think of was Craig. He would have never known if he hadn't told him. Why did he think that being honest was going to make everything all right? Was Craig supposed to pull him into his arms and say that he was sorry that he was sick and tell him how much he loved him? Silas knew the answer to that question as soon as he thought it. He just thought that this one time would be different. But it wasn't. He was alone, again. He lit an incense and pressed play on his CD system. In seconds, D'angelo was echoing through his loft apartment. He took a deep breath, closed his eyes, and once again sank deep into his couch.

Silas, AKA 'Red', was raised in small town USA. He had learned at an early age that he needed a tough skin to survive in this world. He never thought that three letters would grab him by the throat and cause so much pain. H, I, and V walked into his life and threw him against the wall and choked him. After some time, he let go of the depression, saw his doctors, took his medicine, and maintained his physical activities. Just like all of his friends before him, he knew that it would never happen to him. So what, he slipped a couple of times. Maybe he would where a condom, maybe not. Just stick it in a couple of times and pull out before he ejaculated. It would be OK. It took just one incident to change his life forever. And this is the life he had to endure.

Out of all the nights, he couldn't believe he would run into Wes. Yet, it made it so much easier for him to turn him down. He had met Wes at one of the monthly parties that he was so famous for. They exchanged numbers and hooked up a couple of times, but he just wasn't feeling him at all tonight. The music echoed through his entire apartment as he forgot about Wes and thought of Craig's sexy smile, the taste of his tongue and the way their bodies melted into each other in the rain. Then, he thought about Craig's face when he told him to get out of his car. And he thought about the gun.

"Fuck this shit!! Fuck this mother fuckin' shit!" he said to himself as he got up to fix himself a drink. He took a shot of tequila before his shower. He showered and dressed in some sweats as his stereo played. "Fuck this honesty shit!! Hell, fuck it!" He made himself a few more drinks. Soon, he was feeling the effects of his drinks. He picked up the phone. He pressed the speed dial button. In seconds, he was connected.

"Yo, wassup, dis Red."

"Sup shawty. "

"You got some green?"

"You know I do."

"Roll through, then."

"Bet! Be there in ten." They disconnected. Silas smiled to himself as he walked through his apartment thinking about how the alcohol made him feel. He no longer had HIV. He no longer cared about anybody or anything. He was floating. He began to hum to D'angelo as he asked 'How does it feel?'

"It feels good, nigga!" he yelled as he stood in the middle of his apartment in a white wife-beater tank top, some sweat pants, and his socks. "Hell, yeah!!" he shouted. In minutes, his doorbell rang.

"I'm coming, Dammit!" He looked through the peep hole. It was his delivery. He opened the door. There in the hallway stood this short stocky guy with shoulder length dreads.

"So you invitin' me in or what?"

"Come in nigga." And from that point, they both relaxed and in minutes, the pungent smell of marijuana filled the apartment.

"Yo, man, I hear a lot of cats that get down with dudes are supposed to be fillin' up the city this week."

"Oh shit! Dat's right man. It's fuckin' Pride Weekend or whatever the fuck they call it."

"You gonna' be all out there and shit," asked the stocky guy.

"Hell No, man. But I'm still gonna fuck bout five of 'em!" said Silas as he took a deep drag from the joint and started laughing.

"Dat's the whole point of that shit man. All these niggas come out of the woodworks and shit, bodies all cut up, just to find a good fuck or two for the weekend. Man, it's crazy. But you know what?" he asked as he took another drag. "I live for that shit!" he laughed.

"So we gonna fuck or what, yo?" asked the stocky guy. Silas looked at him, vision slightly blurred, and smiled. He put out his joint. He got up and went to his bedroom. The guy followed. Silas started to take off his socks and suddenly, a vision of Craig jumped into his head. His heart began to race. "Fuck this honesty shit," he said to himself.

The stocky guy took off his shirt. His small stocky body was smooth like chocolate. They both undressed and slid into the bed. Soon, their tongues and bodies were intertwined. Silas couldn't wait to feel his visitors hard, round ass. He went for that first. The guy rolled on top of him, which gave Silas the perfect opportunity. Silas palmed both globes with his hands and firmly pulled him into his own body. Their dicks were rock hard as they grinded into each other. Silas began to moan as did his visitor.

"What do you want, nigga?" whispered Silas, his warm breath teasing his visitor's ear.

"I want you to fuck me," he responded. Silas continued grinding into the guys body. Then, he stopped.

"Let's do it without a condom this time," said Silas as his eyes rolled in the back of his head and he smiled. His guest looked at him and grinned. "You wanna do it raw, yo? I ain't did that shit in a minute, man. You gotta be careful and shit deez days," he said as he looked Silas in the eye.

"Look at me nigga. Do it look like I got some shit?" Silas said with his most honest face, as his eyes slightly rolled around. The guy looked at him and thought about it for a minute.

"Come on man, let's just jack off and shit. I'm fucked up," he said as he grabbed Silas and pulled him close. Silas just shook it off and closed his eyes. He soon felt the guys warm hand on his dick. He began to slowly stroke it up and down. Silas' beautifully straight, red dick was rock hard. He arched his back and moaned quietly as his visitor began to quicken his strokes. In minutes, Silas was bucking his hips and holding on tightly to the guy's back.

"Yeah, nigga. Jack that shit! Jack that shit!" Silas said as he was about to explode. His guest was jacking his own dick as he stroked Silas' and watched the intensity in his eyes. Soon, he erupted on his hand, stomach, and on Silas' body. Silas felt the hot streams land on his stomach and this drove him to his point.

"Yeah, shoot that shit! Damn, yo….Damn yo….Im cummin'…Yeah nigga, yeah., yeaahhhhhh…." With those moans and groans, Silas was shooting his juices everywhere. He pulled the guy's hand away, and continued jerking with his own hand. Streams of white cream continued spraying everywhere. One stream brushed across his visitor's cheek.

"Damn, nigga, shoot that shit!" his guest said as he massaged and rubbed Silas' thighs and balls. In minutes, both men were asleep. They didn't get up to clean up or take a shower. They laid there in their sex solution with their minds swirling in clouds of smoke.

21

William's heart raced as he laid there beside me. It was all good at first, but slowly his stomach began to turn. His mind started to spin. He started to shake.

"What the fuck am I doing?!!" he barked as he jumped up from my embrace. "This shit ain't right!" He began to pace back and forth as I sat on the edge of the bed, now up, alert, and staring at William in amazement. I felt it best if I just sat there in silence. So, I did.

"I fuckin' kissed you, man.!! I kissed you back, Craig. I don't believe it!"

"Did you like it?" I asked quietly.

"I ….I…don't know. I just don't know." Yet, he knew. He knew alright. It felt as natural as hugging me. But, he would not let me know that. I knew he had more important issues to deal with, so I decided not to press the issue.

"Hey, you want me to leave?" I asked. William couldn't even look me in the eye. With his back turned, he responded, "I just can't deal with this right now."

I wasn't upset. I understood. Besides, I knew that if William would kiss me, he would eventually do more. I put on my shoes as William stood silently in a far corner of the room with his back towards me.

"I'll return your clothes later."

"Don't worry about it man." In seconds, William's door closed as I left.

"Damn!" said William.

I entered my apartment dressed in borrowed clothes. Once again, I was alone with silence. My heart grew heavy and my throat tightened. I took a long deep breath and decided that it was time to call Mamma. I inhaled deeply one last time as I picked up the phone and dialed the numbers. She picked up in two rings.

"Hello?"

"Hey Ma', what's goin' on?"

"Hey baby, I was thinkin' bout you. You know if we don't hear from you we think that everything is alright. So

68

dat's why I don't call you. You know I be wantin' to. You doin' alright?"

"Yeah, Ma', I'm fine. I hadn't talked to you in a few days, so I was just checkin' in."

"Oh, okay. Everybody doin' good. Yo daddy in the kitchen eatin'. You wanna talk to him?"

"No, that's alright. Just tell him I called."

"Oh, okay, baby. You sho' you alright?" I took a deep breath, closed my eyes, held back the tears and responded.

"Yeah, Ma' I'm fine. Well, you know these long distance calls ain't free. So I better go."

"Okay, baby."

"I love you Ma'"

"Love you, too, baby…..Call us!"

"I will, Ma. Bye."

"Bye Craig." And the line was dead. I hung up the phone and sat there. I cried. I laid across my bed and closed my eyes. My tears began to dry in the corner of my eyes. Soon, I was asleep. Darkness.

22

There I stood, on the top of a mountain. The sun was shining so brightly that I had to shield my eyes from the rays. Suddenly, the ground below my feet began to tremble. In three places, the soil began to sink. Where the sun was, a dark cloud took its place. Thunder and lightening made me blink. As I tried to regain my vision, three figures emerged from the holes. From the first hole emerged William. From the second emerged Wes. And from the third emerged Silas. All three men were completely naked. They all looked up to me with outstretched arms. In unison, their voices began to chant: "CRAIG…CRAIG…..CRAIG….CRAIG!"

"Leave me alone! STOP! Leave me alone!" I yelled. "NO…no….noooooo!" I jerked up.
I sat there at the edge of my bed in a cold sweat.

"Shit, what in the hell was that?," I said as I stood up and walked over to my full length mirror. I thought to myself about all that has happened in my life in such a short period of time. Maybe a hot shower would relax me. I stripped down and started the water for my shower. I stepped in. As I stood in the stream of hot water, I remembered the first time that I brought myself to climax with visions of William in my head. But I couldn't do it now. Or could I? Silas had left my mind. I needed to get the situation out of my head. I was fine. I would be just fine.

I began to lather up and before I knew it, my dick began to stiffen. With my lathered left hand, I stroked it just once. I didn't realize that this would send a wave through me. I tilted my head back and dropped the soap. Not only did I have William's body to imagine, but I now had lips, tongue, taste, smell, and a sexual embrace. I closed my eyes and rolled my head around. I subconsciously began to moan. One of my hands left my dick and began to massage my chest and nipples. I began to breathe deeply and move my hips, still stroking my rock hard dick with the other hand. I knew I needed this private session, but I didn't know if I could handle climaxing. This one might be too much.

"Yeah….yeahhhhh….Yeah, William," I moaned as my dick slipped and slid between my fingers. "Oh shit!…oh shit!….Ohhhhh….ahhhh…" I began to lose my balance. I tried to regain my step, but I stepped on the bar of soap. Before I could catch myself, I was halfway down. I fell with a loud thud as my head hit the side of the tub, with my head just above the tubs edge. The stopper closed down and the tub began to fill with water. I was out cold. In seconds, blood began to trickle down the side of the tub and blend with the warm water. I was unconscious. The water continued to run all over my limp body. The blood continued to flow. Torn away from the world for this moment, nothing mattered. I lay there, silent, alone, beautiful, homosexual, strong, afraid, confident, powerful, helpless, yet, still a man. A black, gay man with the weight of the world on my shoulders. But now, nothing mattered. William was now blackness. Wes was now blackness. Silas was now blackness. Sex didn't matter. Love didn't matter. Nothing mattered. The water mixed with my blood. My world was now on pause.

William was snapped out of his trance when he heard a loud thud above his head.

"What in the fuck was that?" he asked himself as he looked up towards his ceiling towards my apartment. He stood up to find his shoes. He stopped himself. "What am I doing? He probably just dropped something. What I look like goin' up there just because I heard a noise?" So he went into his living room and sat on his couch. He flipped on his television. Without paying any attention to what was on, he mechanically flipped through the channels. He again thought of Craig. He looked up again as he pressed the mute button on his remote control. Silence. He slightly heard what he gathered was running water.

"He's aite. He's taking a shower." He turned the volume back on as he now felt relieved that everything was okay. He sat back and replayed the kiss in his mind. "Damn, it was just like kissing a girl and shit. But I ain't gay. I just can't be." He shook his head and tried to watch TV. Soon, he dozed off. The television watched him as he began to fall deeper into sleep. He left the conscious world and entered the subconscious. He now stood in a desolate desert. He looked all around him and saw nothing but dry land. The sun's rays beat down on his back as he soon realized that he was totally naked. This bothered him at first, but realizing that there was no other human being for as far as he could see, he forgot

71

about his nudeness. Suddenly, in the distance, a form was in motion headed in his direction. He shielded his eyes from the sun as he tried to make out the person. The form began to gain speed as it appeared to be running towards him. He squinted to try and figure out just who this was running towards him. The person got closer and closer. Just as William thought he knew who the person was, the ground began to tremble. Suddenly, the earth opened up and split. The form that William figured to be Craig, could not stop himself. Just where the ground opened up, his left foot went over the edge first. William's heart raced as he saw his friend get swallowed up by the earth. William could not yell or even move. All that he heard was Craig's pitiful cry: "William!!!!!!!! Help meeeeeee!!!!!"

William immediately jerked up. "Oh shit! What a fuckin' dream," he said to himself. Then he realized it was quiet. His television was on mute. He must have rolled over on the remote. Then his mind started to turn. He began to think. Craig's cry for help seemed too real. He sat there in silence, listening for him to yell again. Silence. This unnerved William. He listened. "Damn, he still can't be taking a shower," he said as he heard the water running. He looked up at his ceiling and noticed a wet spot forming. "Oh fuck!" he said as he jumped up to put on some shoes. In minutes, he was up in front of Craig's door, knocking like a maniac. "Craig! Craig! Open the door, man! Open up! It's me, William..........Craig!.......Craig!" Then suddenly, a terrible vision entered his head. The site of a teary-eyed Craig laying in a bath tub of bloody water with his wrists slit. Immediately, he rushed the door. The hinges snapped off! "Craig! Craig!...Where you at, man!" he shouted as he ran straight for the bathroom. He turned the corner and saw the sight he dreaded the most. There I was, unconcious in the bathtub. I lay there silently as the water ran over my entire body. The water was now completely red. William's heart began to race, his throat began to tighten, and tears began to form in the corners of his eyes. "Craig!!!! No!" he yelled as he kneeled down by the bath tub. The water began to run over his body as he grabbed my wrists to see how bad I had cut myself. But there were not cuts. He gently tried to lift me and as he touched the back of my head, he found the source of the blood. He reached for a towel and pressed it against my head.

"Come on Craig....come on man," he said as tears ran down his beautiful masculine face. "Don't leave me, now....Come on Craig, wake up man. You started a lot of shit in my life...and now you trying to leave....You can't...you can't do this to me, Craig. You just can't. Come on, Craig. Wake up....Don't do this to me... I .....I.....I....I need you, Craig. Damn it, I need you! And I don't know what the fuck I'm saying. I'm going crazy. Come on man," he said as the tears flowed and mixed with the running water from the shower. "Just don't fucking leave me to deal with this shit on my own, Craig. I need you. Is that what you wanna hear? Is that it?"

My eyes slowly opened. "Yeah, William, that's it. That's what I wanna hear?"

23

Silas was awakened by the sound of his phone ringing. He rolled over to look at the caller I.D. It was Wes. He rolled back over and faced his sleeping guest. Their sex juices had dried into a crusty substance that stuck to his chest and stomach. Silas got up and jumped in the shower. It was almost noon. Meanwhile, his guest slowly rolled over. He heard the shower water running. He jumped up from the bed and slipped into his boxers. He walked around the bed and searched for Silas' pants. Finding the pair of pants that Silas had on earlier in a pile on the other side of the bed, he picked them up and searched the pockets. He felt the bulge in the back pocket and removed Silas's wallet. Removing three hundred dollar bills, two fifties, and a couple of twenties, he wiped Silas out. He fumbled around for another minute or two. In seconds, the guy was dressed and out the door. Silas stopped the water, dried himself off as he looked in the mirror. He closed his eyes, took a deep breath and opened them again to face himself. Nothing changed. He wrapped the towel around his waist and walked back into his bedroom. His bed was empty.

"Corey! Where you at, yo?" he called out. No one responded. He was nowhere to be seen. Silas' heart began to race. He immediately looked around to see if anything had changed. Nothing appeared to be moved. Then, his pants in the corner caught his eye. "Oh shit," he thought as he ran to get his wallet. Empty! His heart dropped. His rent money was gone. He ran out into the breezeway of his apartment. His visitor was no where to be seen.

After making love to Craig in the pouring rain, he vowed to himself that he would never sell himself again. He was now in a compromising position. He had no extra cash and rent was due yesterday. This time, if he was late, the proper authorities would definitely boot him out of his home. He sat down on the edge of his bed as he held his now worthless pair of pants in his arms. The musty smell of marijuana and sweat entered his nostrils. He just couldn't believe he was robbed. He had only hung out with this supplier twice before this particular visit. So he had no idea if he would ever run into him again. All that he had was a pager number and he knew that the rogue wouldn't respond to any of his pages now. He didn't even know if Corey was his real name.

"Shit!! What was I thinking leavin' that motha fucka in my room! Shit!" he said as he threw his pants to the floor. He was desperate. He had nowhere to go. He knew what he had to do, no matter how much he knew he would regret it. He went over to his phone and dialed some numbers. In seconds, he was connected.

"Hello?" the person answered.

"Wassup yo? Dis Red."

"I know who this is, even if that ain't your name on my caller ID."

"Oh, you got jokes now, huh?"

"You know I'm just messin' with you, Silas. Do what you got to do to reach out and touch somebody, even if it means usin' somebody else's name," he laughed.

"Yeah, yeah, yeah."

"What do you want Silas?"

"You, Wes."

"Why you playing with me, Silas," asked Wes.

"I know I was kinda hard on you earlier, but that was because I was protecting myself."

"What do you mean, 'protecting' yourself?"

"I don't know. I just kinda told myself that I wasn't gonna fuck around anymore. You, know, be cool and just chill and shit. But I was here all last night thinkin' bout you, yo. Just seein' you again brought a lot of shit back," He said and paused, choosing his words carefully. "Damn, Wes, it is good when we get together, you know that," he lied as he rolled his eyes.

"Yeah, I know. It's damn good," smiled Wes.

"So what's up?"

"You need me to come get you?"

"Yeah, if dat's cool with you."

"So….what we gonna do when I see you?" asked Wes.

"Shit, I'm ready to freak yo. I'm down for whatever," said Silas, now smiling at how talented of an actor he was.

"No, tell me what we gonna do, Red." Silas got comfortable. He had played this game before and he was good at it. He leaned back and cleared his throat. He closed his eyes. This time he put an image of Craig in his head.

"Yo, Wes, I'm gonna put it like this, you ain't gonna be able to do anything without thinkin' bout my shit. When we get back to your place I'm gonna stick my tongue deep in your mouth, tasting every corner as I suck on your tongue between every lick. Then, I'm gonna make my way down to your nipples"

"Yeah, Red, yeah nigga," moaned Wes.

"Then I'm gonna lick on each of those nipples, and bite them motha fuckas, yo, while I take my hands and grab that tight ass and pull you close to my hard dick. Then I'm gonna grind this hard dick into yours as I open up that ass with my fingers, get that shit ready. Then, I'm gonna lay you down on the bed and eat that ass. Then, just when you ready, I'm gonna slide this big dick in and fuck you like last time."

"That's what I'm talkin' about, boy. I took today off, so let me get things cleaned up here and then I'm on my way," Wes said as he hung up the phone.

Silas sat there and started stroking his beautiful red dick. In his mind he was once again making love to Craig. He closed his eyes and started to moan and whisper Craig's name. He could feel Craig's warm ass wrapped around his dick. He could taste the mixture of vanilla oils and rain water on Craig's neck. He could feel Craig's warm, wet ass cheeks slapping against his toned, hard thighs and hanging balls. But he had to focus on the present and focus on Wes.

Wes drove to his empty condo that he often used for his sex trysts. They had only been in the house for thirty minutes and were already semi-naked. Silas stood there in some sexy navy boxer briefs and Wes in some black silk boxers. His muscular thighs were pressed against Silas as their lips devoured each others'. Wes' muscular chest pressed against Silas' toned body so deeply that they became one. Wes began to grind into Silas' body as he slowly squatted. His tongue made its way down Silas' entire body. His nose brushed through Silas' pubic hair. Soon, Silas' entire dick was in Wes' mouth. Silas closed his eyes and grabbed the back of Wes' head as he forced his entire shaft into his mouth.

"Yeah nigga. Suck that shit...Damn Wes...Damn, nigga...yeah...yeah....," growled Silas. Wes moaned as he

closed his eyes and rolled his tongue around the head of Silas'
dick. He then started to lick Silas between his thighs and
around his balls. This drove Silas crazy. He was ready to
fuck. He grabbed Wes' head and pulled it back.

"Lay on the bed on your stomach," he forcefully said.
Wes just smiled and stood up to remove his boxers. In
seconds he felt Silas hands massaging his thighs. Soon Silas'
hands were on his ass. Then, just what he was waiting for, he
felt Silas' wet, hot, firm tongue deep in his ass. He squirmed
and moaned as Silas went deep and hard with his tongue.

"Can I fuck dat ass, Wes? Huh, can I fuck dat ass?"
he whispered.

"Yeah, nigga fuck dat shit," Wes responded. In a
matter of minutes, Silas was covered and lubed and fucking the
hell out of Wes' hot, muscular ass. He was pounding the hell
out of it. Their sweaty bodies slapped and slid forcefully
against each other. They were going hard and fast! Wes was
moaning and enjoying every minute of it. Suddenly Silas
stopped.

"Shit, the condom broke!"

"Don't worry about it nigga, keep goin. Keep goin,"
pleaded Wes. Silas closed his eyes and slowly picked up his
rhythm again. Soon, he was at full speed.

"I'm bout to cum, yo.... I'm bout to fuckin nut, yo!"

"Yeah, Red....Let me feel that shit. Go ahead, yeah,
boy shoot that shit!" Before he could withdraw, he was
shooting hot streams of cum deep into Wes ass. He wanted to
pull out, he really did, but it was too late. It was too late. It
was too late.....

77

24

I looked into William's eyes. He had just told me that he needed me and I had responded. William was thrown, but had no time to reply. He immediately stopped the running water.

"Hey, man, we need to get you some help. Can you move? NO! Don't move! You're not supposed to move somebody with a head injury," he snapped as he tried to hold me down.

"No, William, that's for neck injuries. It's my head, not my neck," I said, drowsily.

"It doesn't matter. Just don't move. Here, hold this right here," he said as he reached and handed me a towel to place under my head. "I'll be back. I'm callin' the ambulance." He disappeared into my apartment. I just laid there holding the towel behind my head. I couldn't believe it. I was lying in a bath tub with a bleeding opening in my head and all that I thought about was that William had come to rescue me. Then, I began to think deeper about the situation, something I always seemed to do.

"Maybe he said it just because he thought I was dying. Did he really mean it? Did the kiss really mean something to him? I heard him say it, God. I heard him say it. He said he needed me and that's all that matters," I finally said to myself. At that moment, I began to get dizzy. Suddenly, all that I saw was blackness. I was out again.

When I slowly opened my eyes, I saw the bright lights of a hospital ceiling. I blinked and tried to focus on my surroundings. It was pretty quiet except for all of the beeping machines that were connected to me. I looked to my left and saw monitors, wires, tubes, and a portrait of lilies in a field. I slowly turned my head. I got a little dizzy. So I stopped, closed my eyes, blinked a few times and tried it again. I slowly turned to the right this time. My heart got heavy as I smiled. There, spread out with his arms folded across his chest, was William, asleep. I just stared at him and watched him sleep. There was a powerful, beautiful, black man sitting in my hospital room. I thought about the first time that we had embraced. I thought about how secure and how safe I felt in his arms. Then I remembered William had said that he needed me. I smiled again. Suddenly William began to stretch out and yawn. He was waking up.

"Oh, now you watching me sleep," he questioned as he stretched. "What happened? I leave you alone for two minutes and I come back and you knocked out." Finally, he got up to walk over to my bed. I just smiled and blinked to acknowledge him.

"Yeah, you scared the hell out of me, Craig. Don't do that shit again, aite?" I lightly knodded as I turned to face the ceiling again, and closed my eyes.

25

Wes and Silas lay there in their own after glows; two different after glows. Wes, laid back on one side of the bed, feeling completely fulfilled. Not too many knew that he received dick as well as he gave it. In fact, Silas was the only guy that he would let penetrate him. To everyone else, he was a top. He had finally caught his breath and was totally relaxed. He just laid back smiling to himself. Silas was on his side facing the opposite direction. He pretended to be asleep. But his mind was far from being at rest.

What had he done? He knew! He knew that he was infected! He knew that he should have stopped when the condom broke. He knew! The thought had indeed crossed his mind, but it felt so good! Maybe, deep down, he felt that Wes needed to suffer his pain. Soon, however, his logic kicked in.

"Yo, Wes?"

"Yeah, what's up Red?" he asked with a hearty grin.

"Yo, do you ever get tested?" Wes' smile immediately disappeared and turned into a face of concern.

"Hell yeah I get tested! Do you?!?"

"Yeah, I get tested," Silas replied dryly.

"Wait a minute, Red. You trying to question me, like I'm the one who's gonna give you some shit? I should be questioning you! You're the one that's all out in the streets and shit!" Silas just lay there. He couldn't believe that Wes took his question as an attack. He said nothing.

"You hear me? Silas?...Silas?" He was in his own zone. By the time he snapped back to reality, Wes was getting up to take a shower. He was mumbling something about Silas questioning him about being tested. Silas sat up in the bed. He was still naked. His limp dick just rested on the bed between his legs. Immediately, an image of Craig's rain drenched face flashed before his eyes.

"Where you at, Craig? I will probably never see you again," he said to himself. The water started to run as Silas sat on the edge of Wes' bed. There, on the nightstand was Wes' wallet, where he always left it. Visions of Craig left his mind as thoughts of rent entered. For two minutes straight, he stared at the wallet.

80

"Fuck this shit," he said to himself. Silas believed that God worked in mysterious ways. Was this one of those times? He knew that he needed his rent paid. He slowly walked over to the nightstand. Kenneth Cole was embossed in the lower right corner. It was a nice leather wallet. Silas picked it up and found about five hundred-dollar bills, a couple of twenties, and a five. He cautiously removed two of the hundreds, closed the wallet and placed it perfectly back onto the nightstand. His heart raced with fear and excitement. Shit, his rent was going to be paid. He knew he could get the rest elsewhere. It was definitely time to get the hell out. He quickly jumped in his pants, threw on his shirt, and held his boots in his hands. He waited until he heard the water completely stop.

"Yo, Wes?!"

"Yeah?" called out Wes from the bathroom.

"Hey, I'm bout to bounce! I'm gonna catch the bus."

"Yeah....close the door behind you!"

"I will, yo. I'll hit you up lata!" Wes didn't answer. There was no need to respond. Silas was already gone. He finally shook the thought of Silas' questioning him and smiled to himself as he dried off.

"That little red punk gonna ask me if I get tested. Now ain't that some shit," he said as he wrapped the towel around his waist. He walked into his bedroom and immediately noticed that something was wrong. His wallet was open and laying flat on its side. He slowly picked it up and opened the compartment that held bills. He counted. He closed his eyes, sighed deeply, and smiled.

"Hmmm....two hundred? I guess he was worth it."

As I lay there in the hospital in a deep sleep, William stood over me and watched my chest slowly rise with each breath. He thought of how he felt when he found me lying limp in the shower. He wouldn't tell me what he thought I had done to myself. He couldn't. He shrugged it off and just continued staring at my resting body.

"What is all this about, man? Shit, I don't even fuckin' know what to do any more. But I think you know what you doin'. I'm not gay, Craig. I can't be. I can't be, Craig. I just can't be," he said to himself as he looked at me.

I laid there totally oblivious to the world and time passing me by. William was still standing over me shaking his head and sighing deeply.

"I'm goin' home, man," he whispered as he grabbed my hand and squeezed lightly. He collected himself and walked towards the door. He stopped and turned around.

"I'll see you tomorrow, man," and he was gone. I breathed lightly as all of the machines beeped around me. I didn't know that William had left. I was conscious of nothing. Soon, the door quietly opened. My nurse came in. She lightly tapped me on the shoulder.

"Hey baby? Hey..It's me, nurse Greene. Its time to check your stats again." I turned my head slowly and smiled to acknowledge her.

"I got some good news and some bad news, baby," she said as she held my arm to check my pulse.

"The bad news is that I'm gonna be leavin you, soon. They need me over at the Children's Hospital. And I love my babies ovah there. So today is my last day here with you."

I just stared at her in silence, listening closely and carefully.

"But I got some good news for you, though. She's a pretty young thing and she'll be here in a few minutes, so fix your self up and get ready," she said as she lightly patted me on the shoulder. She laughed to herself as she walked out of the room. I just laid there and stared at the ceiling. That was the last thing that I needed, some young attractive woman trying to hit on me and trying to 'bring me to the other side'. I would just be straight with her and tell her straight out that I was gay, so she need not waste her time. As I turned this thought over in my mind, the door slowly opened.

82

"Hellooo? Knock, knock!" said a sexy voice in a playful tone. "I'm your new nurse." She walked over and looked down at me. She couldn't see my entire face with the tubes and the gauze on my head. My eyes were closed as I tried to pretend to be asleep. Her expression and tone immediately changed once she thought that I was asleep.

"Good, you're asleep. I thought that I was going to have to come in here and entertain you. Anyway," she said as she straightened my blanket and tucked it in, "My name is Cicely Rice, your qualified nurse. And when you wake up, you better not be trouble, cuz you won't want it!" she said with a snap of her fingers and a sly grin.

I continued to pretend to be asleep as I thought crafty thoughts in my mind: "This bitch ain't ready." I slowly opened my eyes. Her back was turned as she checked her make-up in a nearby mirror. She continued talking; unaware that my eyes were on her. She slowly turned to walk back towards the bed.

"Yes, sir, I am not going to be the one and you are not going to......."she gasped as her eyes met with mine.

"You're awake!" My eyes swelled to the size of golf balls. My heart began to race. The machines began to go crazy. Cicely still didn't recognize me. She merely gasped because she feared that I had heard everything she had just said. The machines were still going crazy! Soon the other nurses rushed into the room.

"What is it? What's going on, nurse Rice?"

"I...I....I don't know. I...I ...just looked down at him and he just looked like he had seen a ghost! And his pressure...and heart rate...just shot up!"

"Uh-oh, you did it again! I told y'all about hiring these pretty young girls. These boys can't take it! Get her out of here!"

Cicely raced out into the hall and stood against the wall.

"What have I done? He heard me!!! He heard me!!"

In the room, the nurses tried to comfort me.

"Calm down baby!! Calm down...relax....relax..." said the nurse as she held and patted my hand. "Come on, now...it's alright...It's alright... Breathe....breathe..." she said as my chest continued heaving up and down, trying to gain control. Soon, my stats were back to normal.

"Well, I guess she was too much for you to handle, huh? Your pressure shot up like you hadn't seen a girl in years," chuckled the nurse. But she didn't know that this nurse Rice was the same woman that I could have choked to death for calling me a 'faggot' in William's apartment. This was the same girl that walked in on me embracing William. She was the one and the sight of her shocked the hell out of me. I could give a damn whether or not if she was pretty. I would not have some homophobic, conniving, jealous, bitch tending to my medical needs.

"Now you get some rest baby and we gonna get you a new nurse," she said as she finally felt that I had calmed down. She left the room and found Cicely standing against the wall.

"It's okay baby. He was just a little shocked at how pretty you was. He wasn't ready for all that you got goin' on," joked the nurse. All that Cicely could do was force an uncomfortable smile.

"Now you stay out of his room before you give him a heart attack," said the nurse as she walked away. "Go see the patient in Room 314."

Yet, Cicely could not walk away. She had to get to the bottom of this. She collected herself and prepared to go back in. She breathed deeply and she slowly turned the handle. I was wide awake, but resting and trying to relax. I couldn't believe it. And just then, my door squeaked open.

"Hello?..It's me again. Don't look up!! Just let me apologize for what I said...I was just ... talking..."

"Get the hell out of my room before I call security," I said weakly, but with enough force to be taken seriously. Cicely was shocked. She didn't think that what she had said was so horrible that I needed to call security.

"What?....but....but...I'm your nurse. I've got to take care of you."

"No you don't. I want another nurse," I said firmly.

"But...but...I'm sorry, I didn't mean anything I said...I was just being me and speaking my mind." Cicely was usually a powerful woman who stands her ground. But when it came to her career, she would do anything to make it stable. She was let go from her last position because of her attitude. She was not about to let that happen again.

"So you didn't mean it when you called me a faggot?" Before Cicely could respond, the intercom announced that she was needed in ER.

"What...what...I never said that...I...I..." Just then, the door opened and it was Nurse Green.

"Didn't they tell you not to come in here again! Didn't you hear them callin for you in ER?!!"

"Yes...yes, Ma'am, yes ma'am," she responded with a confused look on her face, glaring at me. And she was gone. I just closed my eyes and shook my head.

26

Silas got off of the bus and walked from his stop until he made it to his apartment. He went directly to his leasing office. He put his money into one of the envelopes that they provided and put it in the night box. It felt as if a burden was lifted. Yet, he still faced another problem. Had he infected Wes? He thought that it wouldn't bother his conscience, because maybe Wes deserved it. But it wasn't his power to give someone a death sentence, he soon reasoned. He turned the lock of his door and was once again greeted by the silent loneliness that he knew so well. He looked to see if he had received any calls. There were none. He sighed to himself and tried to sort out his mess. He went in and sat on his bed. He grabbed his remote and pressed play. In seconds, the solemn voice of Nina Simone filled his apartment.

"Damn! Why have I been dealt this hand?" He looked around his empty apartment. His heart grew heavy. Even though he was a strong man, he was still a human being with human feelings. Getting high was out of the question. His number one supplier had really flipped the script on him and stole all of his cash. The only other thing was alcohol. He knew that he needed to take himself away from the situation. He went to his small bar to see what he had.

What in the hell is this shit?" he asked himself as he reached for a small glass bottle. The label was worn off, but the bottle was half full. He took a whiff.

"Damn!!! This is just what the doctor ordered!" he laughed as he poured some of the liquid into a shot glass.

"Well, Craig, this is for you, wherever you might be and to Wes, Fuck you mothafucka!" he toasted as he took the shot to the head. This first shot was followed by a few more and Silas eventually found himself almost unconscious. He lay there on a bean bag, his breath light, his body numb. Suddenly his phone rang. He twitched as the sound echoed in his ears. He rolled over to attempt to pick it up. His coordination was gone. He knocked it off the hook.

"Hello?...Hello?....Silas!!!....Silas?.....What's goin' on? You aite?....SILAS!!!" said a voice on the other end.

Silas was out cold. Wes immediately hung up the phone. This wasn't like Silas. Wes was out the door and in his car in minutes.

William made it home, sat down on his couch and clicked on his television. He flipped through all of the channels three times. He could not believe how his life was changing. How could he be gay? How? He then immediately thought about his Uncle Wes. It bothered him to think that all the gay people in the world were probably victims of molestation. That was the only way to explain it. Nobody's born that way, he felt. They had to be abused by somebody to screw up their mind and make them gay!

"Damn you Uncle Wes! Damn YOU!!!" he said as he finally turned off the television. He went deeper into his apartment to his room. He laid across his bed on his back staring at the ceiling. What now? What's next? What's next? He decided to give his mother a call. William dialed the number.

"Hello?"

"Hey Mom, what's goin on?"

"I haven't heard from you in quite some time, son."

"I know, I know, Ma, just been real busy."

"Have you seen your Uncle lately?"

"No, Ma, No I haven't," he lied.

"Well, he lives over there near you, I don't know why you haven't run into him."

"I know Ma' I know. Ma', I need to ask you something."

"What...what is it, William?"

"Has Uncle Wes ever been in any trouble?"

"What....what do you mean, William. Trouble like what?"

"Come on Ma' you know, any legal trouble."

"What's going on William? Why are you asking me that?"

"Has he been in any trouble, Ma'!?" His mother got quiet for a minute. William knew something was wrong.

"Ma? What is it?"

"Well, there was never any truth to it."

"Truth to what Ma'....what is it?"

"Well, there was this boy who wasn't quite right that said your Uncle had touched him."

"What do you mean, Ma?"

"Well the boy was sweet, you know, he was a little sissy. He said your Uncle had done some stuff with him. But there was never any truth to it."

"Do you think he did it, Ma'?"

"What...What?! How can you ask me that?"

"Do....you....think...he....did...it!?"

"It doesn't matter what I think, William, your Uncle, my brother said he didn't do it and I stand by blood. Now don't you go starting any trouble," she said , almost in tears.

"Alright Ma' I gotta go."

"Alright baby. I love you, William!" But William had already hung up.

Wes found Silas unconscious on the floor. He was familiar with the leasing office and got them to let him into Silas' apartment. He got him to the hospital immediately. He now sat in the waiting room as they had just wheeled Silas off to ER, still unconscious, but with a pulse. He reeked of alcohol. He laid there, barley breathing.

"Come on, son, don't leave us yet. Come on. Come back to us, son," pleaded the doctor calmly. Soon, Cicely rushed into the operating room, flustered and suited up.

"Where were you, nurse? We called for you. You were supposed to be here when I got here." Cicely rushed to put on her mask, taking the doctor's harsh words as a tremendous blow.

"I'm sorry doctor...I...I.. was..."

"No time for excuses. What are his vital signs?" At that moment, there ceased to be any. The machine echoed that morbid tone of death: BEEEEEEEEEEEEP!

"Come on now....Come back!!!...Come on back, son," yelled the doctor as he tried to revive Silas. After minutes of trying to recesutate him, they found a pulse. He was breathing again. After a few more tests, they rendered him stable and moved him to a room. He was diagnosed as having alcohol poisoning, but was okay now. Now that he was stable, Cicely had other things to consider. She went to sit alone in the cafeteria. She sat there staring off into space. She did not notice the man that quietly sat down beside her.

"Hey, you aite?"

"Oh...I didn't see you. I'm..fine....I'm okay," she said

"My name is Wes, and you don't look okay."

"Well, I'm fine...just fine, umm, Wes...."

"Come on, you can tell me what's on your mind."

"It's just a lot of crazy stuff going on. I don't want to just tell some stranger my problems."

"Come on, you know me, now. I told you, I'm Wes," he smiled. This brought a smile to her face. She knew that he was trying to make her laugh.

"I'm Cicely, Wes. But wait, before I tell you anything or say anything else, I need to know, are you gay?" Wes almost choked, but collected himself.

"What? Why you ask me that? Do I look gay?"

"I'm sorry, but you just gotta ask that question these days."

"I understand that. My answer is 'No'"
Well he wasn't gay. He was BI-sexual. And she didn't ask if he was BI-sexual. She asked if he was gay. So, technically, he didn't lie. He smiled to himself.

"Well this guy I was um...um...dating, has been acting strangely lately. I think he might be gay. I ....I kinda caught him with another guy and now this patient yelled at me and....." At that single moment, her heart almost stopped. It hit her. Craig's face flashed before her eyes. She remembered his voice.

"Oh my God! I've got to go!" she said as she jumped up and was gone. Wes stood up. He didn't know why this beautiful girl had just got up and left in mid-sentence. Maybe he should go check on Silas now. He made his way through the hospital corridors. He stopped. As he came across the nursery, he noticed a baby. Wes got so close to the window that his nose touched the glass. Suddenly, he was in a trance. He began to think about his own childhood........

He stood there naked in the locker room shower. He had to run laps because he was late for practice. He hated running laps, but it made him stronger. His teenage body was maturing perfectly. His toned calves and thighs glistened as the water ran down his legs. His slightly aroused penis dripped with suds as he lathered himself. He was the star of the football team. He was also somebody else's star. He turned his head as he heard someone entering.

"Hello?...Helloooo?...Who is that?" he called out. There was a few seconds of silence.

90

"It's just me, Coach Miller," said his coach.

"Um..Oh...wassup Coach," said Wesley nervously. Coach Miller was completely naked. He had played every sport known to man, with a couple of years of weight training. His body was solid. His slightly pigeon-toed walk made him seem even manlier. He walked in and stood two showerheads down from Wesley.

"Me and my girl going to a little dinner get-together this afternoon. So I said I would shower here before I got home. You know, speed up the plans," he said.

"Yeah, that's cool Coach," replied Wesley. He was so nervous. He didn't know why he was feeling so weird. It was only his Coach. He had seen all the other guys naked before, but this was Coach Miller, a grown man. He tried to relax and finish bathing.

"I see you take care of yourself like I did at your age," said the Coach with a sexy grin.

"Um...yeah...I...I...like to stay in shape," replied Wes. But no matter what, he would not face Coach Miller. It's a good thing he didn't, because the Coach had begun to slowly stroke his dick.

"Yeahhh, you got a tight little body, Wesley." This startled Wes. He turned to face the Coach.

"What's up Wesley. I can't help it if the Coach is a little horny," he said, now smiling ear to ear. Wes tried not to look down at the Coach's dick, but he knew he wanted to see it.

"Come on, boy. I know you guys play around in here. I did it when I was your age."
Wes just stood there staring while slowly scrubbing his chest.

"Come here, Wesley. Come here and touch it." Wes raised his eyes to face the Coach. He slowly walked towards him. Just inches from each other, the Coach reached out and placed his hands on both of Wes' shoulders.

"Go ahead, touch it. Let's just jack off. I know you and the guys do this shit." Wes slowly reached out his right hand. He made contact.

"Yeah, Wes, yeah boy, rub it. Rub it!" Wes began to slowly stroke it up and down. This sent the Coach into ecstasy. He cocked his head back and squeezed Wes' shoulders.

91

"Yeah boy, yeah Wes, you like that, huh?" Wes did like it. His own penis began to grow. So with his free hand, he began to jack his own dick. The feeling of another man's penis in his hand made him even hotter. In seconds, he was shooting streams of cum on the shower floor. Seconds later, the Coach was moaning. His fluids ran down Wes' hands onto the shower floor. Both men convulsed until every last drop was out. The two stood there still connected and breathing deeply.

"Go dry off son, and let me wash up," said the coach as he let go of Wes' shoulders..........

"Cute baby, huh?"....

"Huh..what..?"

"The baby, that one is mine. Ain't he cute?" said a little black lady in a robe.

"Yeah, um....really cute," said Wes coming out of his trance. He looked at the lady and then back at the baby. He walked away.

Silas was finally conscious. Yet, he felt terrible. His head throbbed, his mouth was dry, his stomach nauseous, and his energy was barely holding on. He heard a knock at his door.

"Knock, knock....Hey baby...It's me nurse Green. How ya' doin', Craig?" she said. Silas heart jumped as he jerked up, adrenaline flowing.

"What?...Huh? What you just call me?"

"Oh my...you ain't my baby. I'm in the wrong room...I'm sorry baby, lay back down,"

"Wait! Is there a Craig here?"

"Yeah, he came in today. He must be next door. Sorry I bothered you." She was gone as quietly as she entered. Silas heart began to race and his mind turned. Could it be? Could it really be? Did Craig have an accident the brought him here? He slowly tried to collect himself. He could barely move, but found the energy to get up. He inched his way to the door. He was out in the hall now as he had disconnected himself from the machines. He walked down the hall to the very next door. He didn't knock. His heart would not stop pounding. He turned the latch and opened the door. There, sitting in the bed before him, was Craig. He had fallen asleep sitting up, while an old episode of The Cosby Show watched

92

him. Silas just stood there staring into Craig's face. He could not believe his eyes. He just couldn't believe it. Now they could finish what they started, thought Silas.

27

Silas just stood there for a couple of minutes in awe. There, before his eyes, was the man that he thought he would never see again. He just stood there. Visions of Craig's rain-drenched face played with his mind. It was just as he remembered it. He was suddenly interrupted.

"Excuse me sir. Are you ok?" asked a nurse from behind him.

"Um. . oh yeah, I'm aite," he said as he tried to stand up straight.

"Do you know Mr. Washington?"

"I...I...don't think I do. I thought he was somebody else," lied Silas.

"Well it's time for his medicine."

"Oh, my bad....I'll...I'm going back to my room," said Silas as he shuffled back to his room, one door down the hall. He slowly lay on his bed and took a deep breath. He couldn't believe it. He couldn't believe fate was working her magic.

28

Cicely rushed through the hallways and to the elevator. She could barely contain herself. Her heart raced! The doors to the elevator slowly opened to Craig's floor. She breathed deeply as she walked down the hall. Halfway down the hall she passed the nurse that had given me my medicine. She stood in front of my door. She took one more deep breath, turned the latch, walked inside, and closed the door behind her, all in three swift moves. She stood with her back against the door.

"I know who you are!" I was caught off guard. My eyes flew open and I just looked at her with a confused expression. "We need to talk," she said.

Finally adjusting to the situation, I got comfortable. I sat up straighter in bed with my arms crossed.

"Talk," I said, simply.

"Are.... you.....gay?" she asked in three dramatic words. I just peered through her. How could she ask a dumb question like that when she had already convicted me of the crime by calling me a faggot? I sat in silence for a few seconds. Then, just as dramatically as she had asked, I responded, "Yes......I .....am, but what does that have to do with anything? That still doesn't give you the right to call me a faggot!"

"Ok, look...I apologize, about that. But I was angry, hurt, and....and, I was jealous. Yes I was jealous. You walk in and see somebody who you had hooked on you like a drug addict in an embrace with another man! It's just hard on a woman. Even more, the other man is just as fine as your man...I mean, what was I supposed to do?"

"Accept the fact that two guys can be friends. Two guys can hang out. Two guys can even hug each other and it not mean anything sexual."

Although I knew that the hug meant a hell of a lot to me, for argument's sake, I played it down a bit. Cicely slowly walked over to my bed.

"So.....Is William gay?"

95

"Come on now, it's not my place to answer a question like that and you know it."

"I know, but it's been eating at me every since...umm...you know. And I know William would kill me if I asked him."

"What do you want from him?"

"I don't know. I don't know. I used to think it was just the sex, but when I'm with him, I feel safe and protected." I thought to myself, "Me too."

"I just don't know anymore. So....have you two ever...ever...messed around?"
I gave her a look that would have burned a hole in the wall.

"I'm sorry, but I just can't get over it all. Are you sure you're gay? I mean, why would you choose to be like this?"

"First, it's not a choice. From as far as I can remember, I have always had these feelings. I was never touched or molested. I was just born this way."

"So you don't want to be a woman or anything, do you?" I laughed so hard that I almost choked.

"Hell No! Why would I want to be a woman? Look, I'm a man. I love being a man. I'm a man first! Then, I'm gay. I just happen to like other men, a lot."

"So how do you tell if a man is gay or not?"

"Ask him for his GAY card," I said with a grin. Cicely smiled too.

"I'm serious. I was just down in the cafeteria talking to this nice looking guy. I forgot his name, Chris, or Mike, or something. Anyway, I just flat out asked him. He said 'No' but how do I know?"

"The proof is in the pudding. You will know. You will and when you do, don't run from it or deny it. Accept it and move on, with or without him. But you will know. And when you know, don't chastise him for being gay, chastise his ass for lying to you!" Just then, she was once again being paged.

"Damn, I gotta go. We'll talk later..." She smiled as she left the room. I couldn't believe it. I knew how bad I hated her for what she said, but something was happening. I felt that I had actually reached her. I smiled. Now, what do I do with William?

29

William had rested and relaxed. He now had me on his mind. He got up and showered. He threw on some clothes and headed back to the hospital. He stopped by the store and picked up a little something for me. He made it to the hospital with an elaborate fruit basket. As he got off the elevator, he straightened his shirt.

"Well, well, well, hello there, stranger," said a voice from behind him. William recognized the voice and almost shit a brick.

"Cicely?! Hey what....what's goin' on?"

"Nothin, Whats goin on with you? Who's that for?"

"Ummm..umm...my cousin...my cousin is sick and, um..he's here."

"Ohhh...okay. Where is he? Is he on this floor?"

"Uhh....DAMN!, I'm on the wrong floor, again!"

"Oh, is that so? Well, walk with me for a second, let's catch up," she said as she linked her arm with his.

"No, I really need to go."

"Come on William, I want you to meet a friend of mine."

"Come on Cicely, I gotta go," pleaded William, as Cicely continued to lead him down the hall. Before he realized it, he was standing in front of Craig's door. Before he could pull away and make up an excuse, the door opened. The nurse that had just checked my stats again walked by the two of them and left the door open. I looked at Cicely, then at William. William stared at me. Cicely smiled ear to ear, arm in arm with William, looking back and forth at both of us. I then stared at Cicely with one eyebrow raised.

"Hey nurse, what's going on?" I asked in a sarcastic tone.

"Look who I found, um...visiting his ...cousin, I think he said."

"Hey, William, what's up, man?"

"Man, I'm aite, how are you?"

"Could be better, have been better. What's up?" I asked. William didn't know if he should continue the game, lie and run away, or if he should bite the bullet and say that he was here to see me. Hell, I'm his neighbor and friend. But he had already lied, so now, to tell the truth, makes the whole situation seem kind of fishy. His mind turned and he began to sweat. Then, it hit him. He took a deep breath.

"This is for you, Craig," he said as he gently broke away from Cicely's arm. Her eyes almost shot out of her head as she held her chest in disbelief. I was caught off guard too.

"Um..Thanks, William. I'm gonna need that fruit for some energy."

"Yeah, you're gonna need energy to deal with me checking on you and your clumsy ass every five minutes," said William as he put the basket down on my bed and jabbed me in the shoulder. Cicely stood frozen at the door. She couldn't tell if we were behaving like brothers, friends, or lovers. Her jealous heart told her 'lovers', but her logical, sound mind said 'friends'. It was like two close friends interacting with each other with love, compassion, consideration, and warmth. She was speechless. Yet, it was still too much for her. She left the room.

As she walked down the hall, she ran into Wes.

"Hey there. What happened? You shot out of the cafeteria like a bat outta hell. What's up?"

"Oh...I'm sorry. There is just too much going on. Too much."

" What is it?" he asked as they continued walking. She stared into space and thought for a minute.

"Nothing...just nothing. I'm just reading too much into all of this. Yes, that's what it is. So, how are you, Chris, you said?" Wes looked at Cicely with a confused look. How could this woman forget his name?

"Wes...It's Wes, Cicely," he said firmly. She really didn't notice his frustration. She was in her own world. The man that gave her some of the best sex in her life was in a hospital room showing affection to another man. Not just any affection, but the affection and warmth that she wanted. She had to stop this thought process before it snowballed. She came back to reality. Standing next to her was a gorgeous man with a body to die for. And here she was losing sleep over a closeted punk and his secret lover, she concluded.

"Hey, Wes? What are you doing later? Maybe we could grab a bite to eat," she said as she looked into his eyes.

98

At first, he was caught off guard, but he quickly collected himself.

"Sounds good, but only if you remember my name," he said with a sexy grin. "Here's my card. Give me a call later. If I'm not there, call me on my cell." Cicely inspected the card and smiled.

"Ok. I will call you, soon." Wes walked away as Cicely smiled to herself. New meat is always good.

30

Silas laid in the hospital bed in bliss. All the thoughts of how he was going to reunite himself with Craig flowed through his head. Would he go over and just apologize and tell him that he wore a condom when they had sex? Or would he go over and beg for forgiveness? Wait! Why should he be forgiven? Craig never asked him if he was infected. Craig was a strong man. He could have stopped him if he wanted to really stop him. Yet, Silas somehow knew that these thoughts did not legitimize what happened. He sat on the bed in silence. His nurse came in, checked his stats and told him that he could probably go home later in the evening. But Silas needed to see Craig before he left. He needed to tell him how he felt. He didn't know if he had the nerve to approach him. It was now or never, he concluded.

He rehearsed in his head over and over what he would say. He would walk in, close the door, and beg Craig to hear him out. He would tell him that he has never felt the way about another man that he felt about Craig, only after meeting him once. He would tell him that he wore a condom that was completely in tact before and after they had sex. He would beg for forgiveness and a second chance. Yes, that's what he would do. As he sat on the bed, a smile covered his entire face. His serene moment was broken as his door knob turned. It was his doctor and another nurse. They carried folders and grim looks on their faces as they slowly walked in.

"Mr. Woodson, how are you feeling today?" Silas didn't know the meaning behind all of this. He just sat up straight with a concerned look on his face.

"I'm aite. What's up Doc's?" They didn't laugh.

"Well, Mr. Woodson. You are aware that you are HIV positive, correct?" Silas knodded. "Yeah...I am. I know I got it," he choked out. "I can still go home, right?"

"We did some additional blood work and discovered that your T-cell count is drastically decreasing. In the coming days, you will be experiencing some drastic changes in your energy level and your overall physical abilities."

"So, what does all that mean? Am I....Am I...dying?" The nurse looked at the doctor for support.

"Well, Mr. Woodson, we are not saying that. It's a little too early to say that. With the right treatment and medicines, we are hoping to slow down any depletion of your systems. But you already know the condition of your kidneys and liver. They really took a blow from your current incident. However, we want you to know, Mr. Woodson, you are in the best institution and will receive the best of care, here, with us. Silas knodded and swallowed.

"Thank you," he mumbled.

"Well, we will be back later with any more updates. Is there anybody you need to call, because you are going to be with us for a few days."

"Yeah, I'll do that later. I just want to chill by myself for a minute," said Silas. The nurse and the doctor nodded in unison and slowly walked out of the room. Silas sat back in bed and took a deep breath. He closed his eyes and for the first time, in six years, he cried. Silas cried. Red cried…

31

William went over to sit in his regular spot across from my bed. He looked at me. I looked at him, both in silence. I cracked a smile.

"So…which room is your cousin in?" I asked. William leaned further back in the chair and stretched.

"He's in room 521, the floor above this one," he replied trying to keep a straight face. We stared at each other for a few seconds. Suddenly, both of us broke out in laughter.

"Man, you are crazy," said William. "You know I ain't got no cousin up in this place. You know how she always getting' up in my business, so I just told her some other shit."

"William… I think she knows."

"She knows what?!" he barked as his comical expression was quickly erased.

"I told her that I was gay."

"What!? Why? Why you tell her that?"

"Because I am!! I'm not ashamed of it. She asked me and I told her."

"What else did you tell her, Craig?"

"What do you mean, William?"

"Just what I said, what else did you tell her?" he asked again.

"She asked me about you and us and…"

"AND WHAT!? WHAT, CRAIG?!"

"Damn, Calm down, William. I told her that she needed to ask you that. It's not my place to tell her about you."

"Why did you say it like that? Why didn't you just say 'NO' Now she got doubts in her mind about me." He stood up and started to pace back and forth.

"This is fucked up. This is fucked up!"

"What's fucked up? What's fucked up, William?"

"You knew exactly what you was saying, Craig. You knew!"

"William?!?"

"Nah, don't fucking say anything else to me, man. I gotta go," he said as he reached for his keys.

"Wait William. It's not like that."

"Whatever man. You want me for yourself so you trying to fuck my shit up. I'm out!" he said as he turned the handle of the door.

"But William…William, I love you !!" Craig shouted.

Just as William walked into the hall, he did not notice Cicely standing at the nurse's desk looking dead at him. Nor did he see Silas as he bumped into him. He kept walking without a word. This didn't phase Silas. Initially, he was on his way to make amends with Craig. However, he now stood frozen in the hallway. He was too stunned to say anything.

32

I could not believe what had just happened. My heart sank deep into my stomach. I did not tell Cicely that William was gay, but I didn't say that he wasn't either. Hell, I really didn't know. All that I knew was that I loved William. I didn't know if William would come back. Just as I was thinking that last thought, I heard a knock at my door. I just knew that it was William coming back to apologize.

"Come in," I said with excitement. The door slowly opened. There standing on the threshold, was Silas in a hospital robe. I could not breathe. My eyes locked with his eyes. I didn't know if I wanted to scream, cry, yell or just jump out of bed and beat the hell out of him. I just sat there, breathing heavily, almost in tears. Silas outstretched his arms. He stood there, glassy-eyed.

"Yeah, it's me. It's me, Craig. I'm standing right here. You thought you'd never see me again, huh? But look! Here I am, Craig. Here I am damn it!!" Tears started to roll down his face. All the while, I sat in bed in complete silence with my jaws clenched and lips pressed tight.

"What? What is it? You want me to leave? You want me to get out? You know what? I understand. I really do and I will. I'm gonna leave, but I need to say something first. I need to tell you something, Craig. I wore a condom, man. It went on and stayed on until I came, Craig." He wiped the tears away from his face like a thug at his homie's funeral.

"And when I did, I checked the condom to see if it was straight before I threw it away. When you got in the car, I checked it and tossed it before I got in, man." I still sat there motionless without uttering a word. Silas paused for a second as his heart became heavy as he thought of the words that he was preparing to say.

"Craig, I never fucked you." I turned my head to one side as if to say "Huh?" Silas continued. "No, I didn't, Craig. I made love to you, man. That night in the pouring rain, when I kissed you, I knew it was good. But when I entered you, I knew that it was right, Craig. With every motion and movement, I became one with you. Not a minute has gone by that I haven't thought about you, Craig. Not one. I know you're okay. You didn't get it."

My doctors had told me already that I was negative, but would need to get tested in a few months. Silas continued.

"But I got it, man. I'm not blaming you, nor am I blaming myself. All that I'm saying is that I could have lied, but I didn't. You know what else, Craig. I'm dying. I'm fucking dying, now. They say my kidneys may not be able to take the stress of all this shit. But, before I go, Craig....Shit, I don't even know your last name. But I do know one thing. I care about you and I will never forget that night. I love you, Craig. I know I do. That's right. I said it! Red said the 'L' word. You ain't got to say shit, man. Because I know you told that other cat you love him. Yeah, I heard you. I hope you happy, man. Just be happy." And with those words, he turned and walked out of my room. I sat there numb. I didn't know what to say nor could I move. So there I sat. I just sat there and I cried too. I wiped away the last few tears. Silas had just dropped a bomb on my heart and mind. How could he love me? It was just sex. It was anonymous, hot, wet sex. I wanted to get up and go find him, but my mind fought against my heart and told me to stay there in bed. Then, I knew. I knew how he could love me. The same way that I loved William.

33

William rushed out of the hospital and into the parking lot. As he reached to open his door, he caught a glimpse of his Uncle just a few cars away, on his cell phone. He slammed his truck's door and started to make his way over to Wes.

"Uncle Wes," barked William. Wes asked his caller to hold on as he looked up and saw William approaching him. He muted his phone.

"Why look who's here! My favorite nephew!" he said with a smirk.

"You can let that shit ride, Wes, Tony, or whoever you might be today," growled William.

"Hey, man, let me call you back," Wes said as he disconnected the line. His jovial expression was now one of hatred. "Now look here, boy, you may not like me, but don't you come over here in my face disrespecting me."

"Oh, like you disrespected me when I was younger? Like making me do that shit that you made me do?" Wes got very close to William, almost touching his nose with his own.

"I didn't make you do shit, Wesley! You liked everything we did and you know it!" Just as William was about to make a fist, the security parking attendant rolled up in his golf cart.

"Is there a problem here, fellas?" Wes looked at the attendant and stepped back away from William. "No sir, no problem at all. Just having a conversation with my nephew, of which I'm done and will be leaving now," said Wes as he got into his car. William stood there glaring at him.

"I will make sure you get what you deserve, Uncle Wes," said William loud enough for Wes to hear. Wes smiled as he turned the ignition and put his car in reverse. He was gone. William stood there and watched him drive off. The attendant slowly rolled away. William's heart beat uncontrollably as his whole face heated up. He got in his truck and also drove away.

Silas, heartbroken, made his way back into his room. He climbed back in his bed and wiped his last tear away.

"Why in the fuck am I crying? This cat don't even feel me and I'm sitting in this hospital bed crying like a bitch when I'm dying." At that point he decided that there was nothing else he could do. The one thing that he thought he could look forward to had shattered before his eyes. He laid back on the bed and closed his eyes. In a matter of minutes, he had slipped off into a state of unconsciousness. His desire to continue had faded away and slowly, so did his fight to live. His kidney had failed and his heart had already stopped. His heart was broken. By the time the doctor and nurses rushed the room, he had peacefully departed.

I heard all of the commotion outside my room. Somehow, I knew what was going on. I closed my eyes and cried until I fell asleep.

34

Cicely helped the orderly get Silas's old room prepared to receive another patient. She now had a new fear. She did not know anyone who had HIV or AIDS. But, being in the medical field, she knew what it could do to you. She now thought of all the times that she had slipped with William and had unprotected sex, or the condom broke. She began to shiver as she again envisioned William in an embrace with Craig. She began to think of all the times that she had sex with William and now wondered if he had been with Craig just hours, or even minutes before her. I lived right upstairs. It would be easy for me to stop by and do it anytime and run back upstairs. She shook her head as she smoothed the sheet and tucked in the corners.

"I will see you tomorrow nurse Rice, "said the orderly helping her.

"Oh....um... ok Thank you for helping me," she replied, snapping out of her trance. She turned off the light and walked down to where I was quietly sleeping. She slowly tip-toed over to my bed and picked up my chart.

"You better not have AIDS," she whispered as she continued flipping through my paperwork.

"EXCUSE ME! What are you doing?" asked a doctor who had entered the room. Cicely almost dropped the charts as she composed herself.

"I....I....um...was trying to see if ...um....I..."

"Now, you know that you are not supposed to be in here, first of all. And secondly, you are NOT to be looking at a patient's chart, especially if he isn't yours. You know I don't like you, Miss Rice, and I will be reporting you to the director," said the doctor as she snatched my chart away from Cicely.

"Now you can exit this room now, or I can call you a personal escort." Cicely glared at the doctor, who wore her hair in a long pony tail and her glasses on the tip of her nose. She rolled her eyes and walked out. I did not hear any of this as I was in a deep sleep. I was dreaming. William had just come to pick me up and take me home to take care of me. Just as I was about to kiss him, Silas walked in and pulled a gun on William and shot him. I jerked up and looked around the room. My doctor was checking on me.

"Hey, Mr. Jackson, it's only me. Having a bad dream?" I finally gathered my orientation and settled back on the bed. I did not speak. I just sat there as the doctor finished checking my vitals.

"Did he die?" I asked.

"Excuse me, Mr. Jackson? Who?"

"The guy next."

"Oh him. Yes, he passed on peacefully. He had some kidney complications." I knew that it was more than that and that she could not tell me. I again closed my eyes. I just wish that I could have said that I was sorry. Forgiveness.

35

William made his way home and entered his apartment. He went straight to his phone. He dialed his mother's number. The phone rang several times and finally the machine picked up.

"Shit!" cursed William as he threw the phone across the room. "That motherfucker don't know who he's dealing with! He just don't know," he said furiously. Slowly, thoughts of Craig crept into is mind. He walked over to the wall where his phone lay. He picked it up and he dialed.

"Craig Jackson's room, please." In a matter of seconds, my sleepy voice answered.

"Hello?" Willliam couldn't speak. His anger was taken away by just hearing my voice.

"Hello??" I asked again, with a little frustration.

"Hey, man. It's me William. I....um....I'm calling to say something that I need to say." I cleared my throat and sat up.

"There is so much shit going on in my life, man. And before anything else goes wrong, I just wanted to say that I'm sorry for the way I acted today. All this shit is so new to me. But the one thing that isn't new, is how you keep crossing my mind. I don't know what it means, Craig. I just don't know. But one thing I do know, I know that I can't be gay. I can't be!"

"You don't have to be, William. Just because you experimented with me and some stuff happened when you were younger, that doesn't make you gay."

"But would me falling in love with you make me gay?"

And with that question, the man behind door 655 had just opened another door. But would he be ready for what was behind this new door, Craig's door. Only time will tell.

Made in the USA
Charleston, SC
20 June 2012